THE POMEGRANATE TREE

Vanessa Altin

ILLUSTRATED B

BLANKET Press

blanketpress.com

THE POMEGRANATE TREE

Vanessa Altin

illustrated by FAYE MOORHOUSE

For Adnan xx
To all warrior women, stay strong,
stay safe – keep fighting… V.A.

For Julip and Sam. F.M.

The author is donating a percentage of her
royalties to the Children's Project of Heyva Sor
– The Kurdish Red Crescent.

The Kurdish Red Crescent was founded in 1993
and has become a beacon of hope for people in crisis.
It is the only aid organisation of Kurdistan.

First published in 2015 by Blanket Press.
Second edition published 2016.
www.blanketpress.com

ISBN: 978-0992872892

Blanket Press and associated logos are trademarks and/or
registered trademarks of Blanket Press.

Text copyright © Vanessa Altin 2015

Illustrations copyright © Faye Moorhouse 2015

The right of Vanessa Altin to be identified as the author
and Faye Moorhouse to be identified as the illustrator
of this work has been asserted.

A CIP catalogue record for this book is available
from the British Library.

Printed and bound in Slovenia.

I. MY DIARY

It wasn't even a proper diary… no dates or days or even
365 pages, it was just an exercise book like you get in school.
I reckon there weren't one hundred pages from cover to cover,
but after this morning I'd be surprised to make it to the end of
the week, so seven pages would be plenty… Well she'd asked
me, told me, in fact, to write everything down. She said it would
help and I trusted her, and as there was nothing else I could
do as we sat in the little courtyard listening to the gunfire in
the streets below us I started to write…

10th October 2014

I am Dilvan. Dilvan from Lanaco*

I stopped writing and poked the end of the biro into the
pomegranate shell and sucked at the juice as I read the six
words over and over and over.
Seeing my name written down made it seem real – official.
I am real.
I am numb.
I am wobbling and I can still hear the whistling in my ears.

* PRONUNCIATION *Lanajo*

I don't know what's real.

Perhaps writing it down will make sense of this strange world that is so familiar and yet changed beyond all recognition.

I stopped sucking the pen and started to write some more…

My name is Dilvan.

That's real.

I'm 13.

That's real.

I'm Kurdish.

That's real.

I've just eaten a pomegranate.

That's real.

This morning my baby sister was beheaded.

Oh God, don't let that be real.

I'm not certain.

I saw her in the line to be beheaded.

I saw the bearded man try to grab enough of her hair to yank her head back and expose her throat – as he had to all the others whose heads lolled around the dusty street.

But, Hira*, that's my sister, isn't even two and she doesn't have much hair – just wispy baby curls and the angry man couldn't get a good enough grip as she wriggled and sobbed in terror – stretching her little chubby arms towards Elif.

Elif's my sister too. She's six and she was in a group being herded onto a truck with my mum and the other women.

Hira was hysterical. She couldn't understand why Elif

* PRONUNCIATION *Hear-ra*

2

and my mum were leaving her – she didn't realise the dirty bearded men with guns were making them.

She didn't see them smash my mum in the face with their gun as she tried to break free to rescue her. My mum slumped to the floor, bleeding, and the other women dragged her onto the back of the truck – leaving Elif torn between her sobbing sister and injured mum.

As the bearded ratman who'd hit my mum raised his gun again to crack Elif on the head, one of the other women quickly scooped Elif up and pulled her into the truck.

I could see the fear and pain in Hira's face – our pretty plump baby whose life, to date, had been lived in a world of love and kisses and clapping games and bee-boo…

In her little pink dress sprinkled with flowers, she was reaching for Elif. She was trembling as the ratman pushed her head into the floor to hold her pudgy little body still and bent down jabbing his dagger into her throat.

Watching from just yards away, safe-ish behind Kurdish lines, the dread of seeing what was left of my family, shattered, bleeding, and now about to be beheaded, my world started lurching, slipping. I was ice-cold but sweating, screaming soundlessly. My mouth tasted of metal. I felt as if my body was turning inside out. I realised I was holding my breath. I couldn't stomach what I was seeing but I couldn't turn away – partly because of Rehana*, the Kurdish commander who was lying on top of me.

She'd trapped me, pinning me with her body, her hand over my mouth as she whispered for me to stay quiet.

If it hadn't been for this warrior woman, I too would have been bundled onto the truck with my mum and Elif to be sold

* PRONUNCIATION *Ray-Hanna*

3

into slavery.

She was saving me – but right now I'd rather be dead. It had to be less painful.

"Hush – shh," she soothed. "Remember God is great. He'll look after Hira, I promise…"

But I didn't want God to look after Hira – I wanted to. I wanted to hold her and hug her and stop her tears and if she was going to die to escape this misery, then I wanted to go with her.

I just had to get Rehana off my back.

Rehana had been one of the best at sports and games in our village – but right now she wasn't playing, and I took the chance to use a dirty trick I'd learnt from wrestling with my brothers. I gasped for breath and let my body go limp as if I'd fainted. Worried she'd squashed the life out of me, Rehana loosened her vice-like grip round my waist and seizing the moment I flung my head back and lashed out with my heels. The back of my head must have caught her face because I felt a tooth dig into my scalp – but the shock and pain for Rehana gave me my chance and I was up and away – scrabbling over the rubble like a goat.

I remember tumbling over the dusty debris and curling my lips back over my teeth – ready to savage the ratman and save my sister or die with her.

And then there was a flash of lightning and it felt, for a second, as if the whole of Lanaco had been sucked into the silence of peace. Just for a second I thought that maybe it was God and maybe he'd finally had enough and maybe he was saving us all…

And that's the last that I can remember of this morning…

2. WELCOME to the COURTYARD

It turns out that it wasn't God – it was a coalition airstrike, called in by Rehana and her Kurdish colleagues to target the ratmen who'd broken into the east of Lanaco early that morning.

It blew me straight off the ridge where we'd been hiding and buried me under the rubble.

Next thing I remember I was lying on a mattress in a courtyard with the sun streaming onto my face. There was a whistling in my ears – everything was blurred and wobbly and for a moment I neither knew who nor where I was.

It was an effort to open my eyes through the crust of grit which was also blocking my nose and clogging my throat.

Slowly the whistling in my ears turned to a buzzing and gradually I realised the noise was the voices of a group of Kurdish fighters squatting under a pomegranate tree in the corner of the courtyard.

Most of them I knew as friends of my brothers. As long as I can remember, my brothers and uncles and cousins and everyone have supported our own Kurdish army – the YPG. We are a proud people

and prouder still of our warriors – and maybe most proud of our fierce and beautiful women warriors – the YPJ. Among them I spotted Rehana.

She was tall and slim, dressed head to toe in combats and with bullet belts slung over her shoulder. Like mine, her long dark hair had been naturally lightened by the sun and she used a red bandana to keep it from her face. She was talking animatedly with the other Kurdish soldiers – and I couldn't tell if they were fascinated by what she was saying or just by her. Rehana definitely had something about her that made her stand out in a group – and as, looks-wise, we were often mistaken for sisters, I really hoped I had it too – whatever it was.

They seemed to hang on her every word, nodding and frowning as she spoke.

Lying in the sunny courtyard, listening to the voices, the trembling in my body eased. I, too, was transfixed watching Rehana. I remembered how she didn't just speak in words – but used her hands and her face to illustrate some important point she was making.

It was warm and I felt sleepy, and as I dozed on my mattress I imagined I was back in our village, watching my mum tend the fruit trees and vegetables she was so proud of. But the memory of my mum in her garden was quickly replaced by the image of her lying bleeding on the back of a truck.

Somehow a sob managed to escape past all the grit and grot in my throat – and as the fearless group of fighters under the pomegranate tree turned to look, the horror of the morning caught up with me and I started to cry.

Rehana spun round to look at me, and my misery turned to shame that made me shiver in the sunshine.

Beautiful, capable and now battered, Rehana sported an ugly swollen black eye and fat lip from my earlier attempts to escape her grip.

Still sobbing, I bowed my head as she strode across the courtyard. She was at my side in a second, soothing and shushing and letting me cry on her shoulder until the sobbing spasms had passed.

We sat quietly then for a while, sipping a glass of hot sweet tea together, side by side in the sunshine, her arm around my shoulders.

"You OK, Dilly?" she asked.

"No," I replied. "Really no... Hira?... What happened? Do you know?"

Rehana shook her head. "Not after the airstrike, I couldn't see anything," she said.

"Look Dilly, we don't have a clear picture of the situation right now. All we know is that they pushed in to the east of Lanaco this morning. That's how come your mum and the girls were taken. They overwhelmed us shelling with their tanks and had over-run the streets before we had a chance to get a warning out.

"If you hadn't been out looking for food they would have taken you too and there's nothing you could have done to stop them, you do know that don't you?" she questioned, tipping my face up to look into hers.

"Yes," I shrugged. I do know, because I have seen for myself how pointless it is trying to stand alone against the ratmen. Their favourite thing is killing – they just love it. The more painful and barbaric the happier they are. Their favourite thing of all is cutting heads off. They are a cruel and whiskered pack, feasting on misery – that's why I call them the ratmen.

"The airstrike has set them back," said Rehana. "The Americans have taken out most of the tanks that were firing on the east and they're hiding the rest now. They've stopped any more coming in to the city – for the time being. Now we're going out to kill those that are left on our streets."

Images of Hira and the smug-faced ratman kept popping in front of my eyes and the rage inside me for revenge was just as strong as this morning.

"I'm sorry for this morning Rehana. I never meant to hurt you but I just wanted to get to Hira," I said, wincing at her swollen face. "Look Dilly, it's OK, I und–"

"I know you don't hate me – I know you get it," I interrupted, "but I realised this morning, watching Hira, that I have nothing left to protect – no one but myself to defend."

"There's nothing and no one left for me now Reh," I rushed on. "When I broke free from you today it was to get to Hira – to save her or die trying – that's what I wanted Reh – that's what I still want now." I was rambling, begging…

"Please Reh – you know I'm strong, you know I can look

after myself and you know I'm a good shot. Please let me come with you. I've got nothing left to lose. Please."

She didn't answer for a minute and I was hopeful... as she hugged me.

Somehow she found a smile from somewhere. "Hey Dilly, that's not exactly true now is it?" and I sensed that she was trying to let me down gently.

"Your mum and Elif are still alive and with luck your brothers will be joining us soon...

"They'll all need that strength of yours Dilly. You have to hold them together, help them – for Hira's sake.

"You have to tell them what happened – and most of all you have to live. These vermin cannot win. We're Kurdish and we will survive.

"I know you're brave and I know you're angry – but you were concussed and your hands are still trembling. You'd be a liability out there right now and worrying about you could get us all killed."

There was no point in arguing – I knew she was right.

"Anyway, there's something more important that you can do while you wait," said Rehana, handing me this exercise book.

"You can write, Dilly. Write it all down. Everything you can remember up to this morning."

"Sit here in the sun. Rest against the wall. It's warm, you're safe and with friends. Write what's happening here."

Tossing me a pomegranate she continued, "Use the pomegranate tree. The sweetness of the fruit will remind you of our life before this," she grimaced nodding beyond the walls of the courtyard. "And the bitterness will remind you of the arrival of the scum in our lives.

"Put in all the details you can – dates, times, descriptions. When this is finished and we've won we'll need records of what happened.

"Even now the world needs to know what's going on. We've got friends, reporters who are desperate to tell our story to the world. They need to know about Hira and all the other children. They need to know what's happening so, God willing, together we can end this. And remember, Dilly – the pomegranate has always been a symbol of hope – as long as we have the pomegranate tree we have hope," she smiled.

I found myself scowling up at her, wondering if there was something wrong with her that she could be so cheerful, positive, smiley even. But I'd known Rehana my whole life and knew that right here, right now – she was at her best. She had never been one for the traditional – she'd shunned cooking and sewing for climbing and shooting. She was patient, disciplined and determined. She loved a challenge and right now she was facing the biggest challenge of her life – we all were – the only difference was she seemed to be thriving on it.

Messages were crackling through on her radio and the others were checking ammunition and loading guns.

"I have to go – for now," said Rehana. "I will be back for you Dilly, but in the meantime start writing," she ordered. So I did.

3. ME

She said to write everything down – so that's what I'll do…
start at the beginning.

I was born in the summer of 2000 in our home in our village of Rojava* which is just a few kilometres from the city of Lanaco.

Although we are in Syria, all of our friends and family think of ourselves as Kurdish first and last – we are Kurds living in our own land which just happens to be in a country called Syria.

Our village, like all villages, had a mosque and a school, and that was about it. We had plenty of land and plenty of friends.

Most of my friends were also my cousins – nearly the whole village is related as most of us marry our cousins – so we end up being just one big family.

Looking back, life then seemed like one long happy sunny day – although at the time I can remember complaining that I was bored and…

* PRONUNCIATION *Ro-shava*

Now I wish I had a rubber. I don't have enough pages to make mistakes. I've just re-read what I've written and realised I have described our village as 'like all villages' which it is in Syria and probably in Iraq and Turkey – but Rehana ordered me to write for the world and I know our village is very different to those in America or England because I've seen them on TV.

So, for anyone who hasn't been to our village – or one like it – I'll try again.

Our village is home to about **(I stop writing and use pomegranate pips to represent the number of houses in our village – and tot up the families in them)** 350 people.

According to my dad, our families have lived in the exact same spot since God created the world, which is a very long time ago.

If you've never been, to get there you'd go past Lanaco, which is a big industrial city right on the border with Turkey.

And with Lanaco behind you it's about an hour's walk towards the rising sun to reach Rojava – depending on whether you have small children with you who complain about the heat, and being tired and the sand flies.

It is hot – most of the time very – except for when it's freezing. It's either boiling or freezing and you just get used to it. I've walked it before with my brothers to our aunties' house.

They live just outside Lanaco and cook kofte and toast and borek and make ayran for the travellers who pass their door.

They sit in their little front yard rolling out dough and stuffing vine leaves with homemade cheese – all things you can carry and eat as you walk – whiling away your journey as you chew on their delicious treats.

Anyway – just past their house you turn off the main road to Turkey onto a dirt track that leads over the hill and down into Rojava.

From the top of the track you can see the whole of our village and beyond – miles and miles of wide open countryside, flat and green and virtually empty. Just the sun glinting on the minarets of miniature mosques in the distance reassures you that life and lunch and laughter goes on in villages, just like ours, all across Syria.

Sitting and looking is a big part of life in our family. Our house is one of the first that you reach in Rojava – higher up the hillside. My dad and his brothers built it before I was born. At first it was just two rooms and a hallway, but over the years my dad has added to it and improved it, so now we have a kitchen, a family room, a guest sitting room (which was very special and kept locked until guests came to sit in it), my parents' bedroom and the large hall that runs through the middle.

The toilet and shower room is on the side of the house but the best bit is the big verandah that my dad built all the way round. This is where we all sit and eat and talk and drink tea and play and watch the world go by.

I stopped writing again for a moment and stretched the fingers in my hand which were stiff – but had finally stopped trembling.

Only me and two injured YPG boys were left in the courtyard.

One had been blinded by shrapnel from a mortar – the other had been shot in the leg by one of the ratmen as he dragged his screaming and sightless friend to safety.

Between them they didn't make one functioning person anymore – one couldn't move, the other couldn't see – so I decided to make them tea and check they were comfortable. But all the while I felt my diary was beckoning me. It was as if just moments before I'd been sitting at home with my family and had just nipped out, and in a few moments I'd walk back in and instead of writing a description, I'd be taking you to meet my family for yourselves.

All the while I was boiling the water and brewing the tea in our traditional caydan (stacked teapots), I kept glancing over at the little exercise book on the ground – half-expecting to see my mum, my home, my whole family intact.

Just writing and remembering had made them all come alive again and it was as much as I could do to serve a glass of tea before snatching up my pencil and diving back into my diary where my family was waiting for us…

As you wind down the hill into Rojava our house is the first one – off the track to the left. The single storey mud and stone house is

whitewashed to reflect the sun's heat, with the wide shaded verandah all the way round. Stairs run up the outside to the flat roof, where we sleep in the summer and from the path you can just make out the mosquito net frames up there.

Behind the house is a raised flat triangle of land, one side hill, one side path, and one side where the land drops away down into a valley with the most magnificent view out across fields and the river below.

Our land, like everybody's, is marked out by sets of stones only two or three rows high. It's not a fence or a wall to keep people out – it's just proof of ownership. From the road it's 151 strides to where the land drops away to the river and it's 284 strides along the top of the drop. Me and my brothers and sisters know every inch of that land. We've walked it, rolled around it, chased chickens and sheep and goats across it. We've helped dig and water it, practised shooting and climbing on it and love it like our own blood.

The house sits right at the back of the plot – away from the road and overlooking our private panorama. When my dad built the extra two rooms, my mum insisted on large windows. Most houses in the village have small windows to keep the sun out – and doing things differently is often frowned upon – but my mum, who didn't much mind being frowned upon, told my dad that the view was God's gift to our home and family.

"Nuri*," she said, "Bigger windows means less building, fewer bricks, less cost and less work for you."

But my dad was more traditional than his beautiful bride and feared being the subject of tea-house tittle-tattle over the ostentatious openings.

"I don't mind the work, Seha**," he told her. "We can have the same windows as my sister has – like your mum's – the new plastic-framed

* PRONUNCIATION *Nu-ree*
** PRONUNCIATION *Shay-Ha*

ones," he offered temptingly.

But my mum was having none of it.

"What is the point, Nuri, in having a tiny window just so we can afford showy plastic frames?

"This," she said gesturing with her arm, "this beauty is God's gift to our home and family. He has created this to lift our spirits.

"Big windows mean at any time we can remind ourselves of God's greatness – it will be a constant inspiration to us and our children – to shut it out behind plastic would be an insult to Allah."

And after that, and in fear of offending Allah, there was nothing much my dad could say.

My dad's brother, a carpenter, had rescued old wooden frames from one of the ancient original French houses he'd worked on in Lanaco – a relic from years ago when Syria was French-run.

So we have big French windows (which did cause much gossip in the village tea-house).

I'm not sure if it was the windows that brought so much joy into our house – or if we were just a happy family or if it just seems like that now.

4. MY BEGINNINGS

I can't remember ever having to describe my family before – everybody in the village knew them way before I was born and we rarely meet strangers so there was no need for introductions, and it feels funny, now, trying to sum them up for you – you, who have never met them and most probably never will.

The sun was high in the sky now and the heat was making my hand sweat and slip as I tried to grip the biro – I popped the pen into my mouth and wiped my hands on my T-shirt to dry them.

As I glanced across the courtyard I realised one of the YPG boys was dozing in the shade of the tree. The other, Rojdan, was staring at his thumbs, lost in his own thoughts. Sensing my stare he looked up and raised his eyebrows at me.

"What are you writing Dilly?" he asked.

"Everything – I'm writing everything," I said – realising, for the first time, how important it felt.

"Rehana told me to – she said it's important that the world knows what's happening here – so that's what I'm doing." I shrugged and turned back to my diary. "Hey Rojdan, how would you describe my brothers?" I asked him.

Slowly a lopsided smile crinkled his face. "Mental," he laughed. "They're all mental – but, God, I wish they were here now," he added.

I nodded in agreement – but didn't speak – picturing my big brothers had brought a lump the size of a plum to my throat and tears were pricking my eyes.

As I bent my head back to my diary the voice of my oldest and most favourite brother, Nuri, echoed in my ears: "Can't play with the boys if you're going to cry like a girl, Dilly…"

I swallowed hard, checked to ensure Rojdan wasn't looking, and dashed away my tears with the back of my hand. No tears, just truth – Nuri was right – if I started crying I'd never stop and they'd have won. The fury that ignites in me when I think of the ratmen spurred me on and I started scribbling furiously again…

So. My family – well first there's my dad, Nuri. He's a big man, with big hands, a big smile, and a big laugh.

I paused for a minute and tried to remember the last time I'd seen my dad – let alone heard him laugh.

I closed my eyes and leant back against the courtyard wall, scanning my memory, reaching back. It was there – I could hear him laughing – I could see his laugh starting from his boots to his belly and spreading from his chin up his face, crinkling his eyes and bursting out from him like the rapid repeat of the machine gun fire we were more used to hearing these days.

Yes, he laughed like gunfire – peppering people nearby with his infectious joy.

He was a clever man – although virtually unschooled. He worked as a vet, and although he had no book learning he had the ability to understand animals. My mum insisted it was his special gift from God – but whatever it was, it was impressive.

I'd watched my dad with animals since I was a baby so it seemed completely normal to me. He used to wear an old brown jacket with leather patches on the elbows and big baggy pockets where you would often find a baby chick or fledgling that he was nursing. His jacket would wriggle and chirp and little heads would pop out of the pockets – much to the delight of me and my little sisters. But as I got older I realised that people from villages miles away would come and ask my dad to look at their sick sheep or cow or horse or chicken – it didn't matter – he had healing hands and could tend them all.

Nobody questioned his gift – in fact there's a saying in our village 'One stroke from Nuri will put a shine on a cow's muddy backside'.

And it was his gift with animals that brought my parents together. My mum, Seha, was the daughter of a shepherd from a village some miles away. Unusually she was an only child – her own mother died in childbirth and her heartbroken father never remarried – choosing instead to take his baby daughter with him to live a solitary existence in the hills with their flock for most of the year.

My mum would often tell us stories of her childhood in the hills – where her friends were the sheep and her family was Grandpa Cevit* and the Kangal dogs he used for herding and hunting.

Syrians don't much like dogs – they use them for work if they have to – and most people are frightened of them. But Grandpa Cevit had learnt

* PRONUNCIATION *Je-vit*

to love them over the years for their loyalty and devoted service.

"Better than a boy – better than a boy any day," Grandpa Cevit would insist to anyone questioning his use of dogs.

"Boys are lazy and troublesome. They get more lost than the sheep and need more looking after – give me a dog any day."

And so it was that he and my mum roamed the hills of the Lanaco Kanton with their prized and powerful Kangals – Xabur* and Bozo.

As a tot my mum would often ride on their backs when her little legs were tired. Standing at nearly one metre tall, the dogs were both bigger and stronger than her, and one of my favourite tales as a child, was of how Grandpa Cevit would strap her onto Xabur's back and she would doze in the warmth of his fur as the pack roamed the wide open countryside seeking grazing for the flock.

I believe those days with my grandpa and the dogs were some of the happiest of my mum's life – but as she grew up her aunts insisted that Grandpa left her with them in the village for school.

My mum said that she loved school, but her face betrayed her and it was clear that she lived for weekends and holidays when she could rejoin her father and furry family in the hills.

* PRONUNCIATION *Shabur*

By the time she was fourteen, my mum had virtually finished school and was back to shepherding by day and camping out with the flock at night.

And it was at night that Xabur and Bozo really came into their own. Wolves, poachers and even bears posed a real threat to Grandpa's sheep – but the Kangals have a natural instinct and a lot of ability to protect their flock.

One night, as my mum slept and my grandpa smoked by the fire, the dogs stood and strained their ears towards the flock. The gentle growling that rumbled from Xabur's throat was a warning to Grandpa Cevit and the sheep alike.

"What is it boy? What can you see?" Grandpa Cevit whispered to Xabur – as Bozo rounded the straggling herd from the higher hills.

Then from lower down the hillside, Grandpa Cevit caught the sound of voices carried to him on the wind. Poachers. Old-fashioned and armed with a blunderbuss, furious Grandpa Cevit set off down the hill to warn them off any ideas of sneaking away with one of his sheep.

The thieves, however, weren't up for a conversation and realising they'd been rumbled they aimed their rifles up the hill to scare off Grandpa Cevit and make their escape. Stumbling and shouting down the hill towards them, Grandpa Cevit had no idea of the danger – but Xabur, with his dog night-vision, saw the muzzle of the rifle glinting in the moonlight and instantly recognised the threat to his beloved master.

Launching himself down the hillside Xabur knocked Grandpa Cevit to the floor as the shot was fired and flew on, teeth bared to confront the poachers.

Firing blindly up the hill the poachers were terrified to see a flying fanged monster hurtling towards them – they turned and fled screaming down the valley – insisting to anyone that would listen to them ever-after – that a monstrous wolf that lived on the hillside could swallow bullets.

Xabur hadn't swallowed the bullet of course but in his rage, he also hadn't noticed when it lodged in his leg.

Only later when my mum had helped Grandpa Cevit back to his feet and Xabur hadn't returned did they realise something was wrong.

In the darkness they couldn't see the drops of blood from Xabur's leg that stained the hillside as he chased the fleeing poachers from his flock.

But it was, in fact, the flock themselves that led Grandpa Cevit to Xabur with their concerned coughing and snorting as they milled around the almost unconscious figure of their leader and protector.

As the sun rose, the sight of her big beast, bloodied and broken, reduced my mum to tears. The realisation that loyal Xabur had sacrificed himself to save Grandpa Cevit made her sob as she stroked his face while Grandpa Cevit, watched by the concerned sheep, worked to stop the bleeding.

And it was this desperate little group that my future dad discovered as he rode across the hills on his rounds.

Aside from the traditional greeting of 'Salam Alaikum' little was said as my dad slid from his horse and watched my grandpa working on his dog's leg.

It was a mess, and as the sun rose and sweat started running down Grandpa Cevit's nose, my dad knelt beside him and started to help. Cleaning the wound, removing the bullet, repairing the damage and fashioning a splint took several painstaking hours – but by the time it was done, Grandpa Cevit, who generally preferred animals to people, had discovered a deep admiration and respect for young Nuri.

For my mum, the love she felt for the man who had worked so tirelessly to save Xabur was overwhelming.

She rewarded him with bright smiles and a hearty stew, and the rest is history. And in one day the great Xabur had saved my grandpa and brought my parents together and secured his place at the centre of our family and our lives.

5. My Family

Within two years from that day my parents were married and my mum went to live in that little house on the hill in my dad's village – Rojava.

Grandpa Cevit took to grazing his sheep on the lush valley beneath their house and between the three of them they provided a home to the flock and all the waifs and strays and unwanted misfits that my dad collected on his travels.

The tradition of caring for sick animals that brought them together continued throughout my parents' marriage and in my lifetime alone, I can remember a duck with no wings (which looked like a tube with a beak and feet), a three-legged sheep and a blind horse – but there were many more.

And before long there were children to join the troupe. I have (or had) five older brothers, two younger sisters and two more that skipped straight from baby to angel – without even drawing a breath in this world.

Oldest and best is my big brother, Nuri, named after our dad. Nuri is twenty-three and everything a brother should be – fun and fair, someone who never lost a fist fight and with a ready supply of sweets for his sisters.

My next brother is twenty-one year old Seladdin, (named after our ancient Kurdish King), who is wise beyond his years.

Next came Azad, nineteen, angry and annoying. Then there's the twins, Barran and Bilal, eighteen years old and identical in everything – looks, likes and learning – and both brilliant with a gun.

Then there's me, Dilvan, thirteen and fabulous! Sweet little Elif who's six and a chatterbox and then the baby, Hira who plonked her little fat self into our family not two years ago, but with such cheerful confidence that it's hard to remember what life was like before she came.

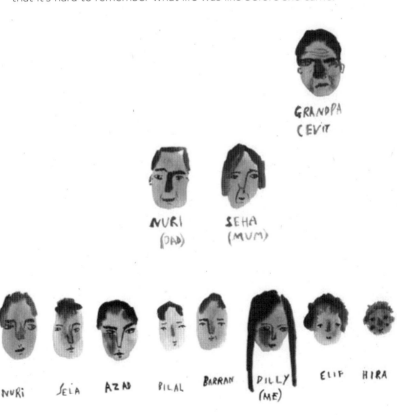

GRANDPA
CEVIT

NURI
(DAD)

SEHA
(MUM)

NURI   SELA   AZAD   BILAL   BARRAN   DILLY
(ME)

ELIF   HIRA

6. VILLAGE LIFE

To us girls, Nuri and Sela were the best big brothers. They were perfect – even though I knew they weren't. We loved them so much that we couldn't bear them to be criticised – even by our parents.

I still remember, with shame, the orange-eating episode – which, at that time, was the very worst, most awful thing that had happened in my lifetime.

I remember it like yesterday although it was eight years ago. I was just five and had started in the baby class at the village school.

School was, in fact, only one room with a teacher (sometimes) and an outside toilet but we were really lucky to have that. Lots of villages didn't have a school at all – some would send their children to our school but others would just send them to work and they would never know the joy of chanting times tables or writing your own name and that's just how it was.

I knew how lucky I was and would go to school with my backpack and my brothers – skipping and brimming with pride.

On the way to school we'd pass the market, run by Uncle Hussein. We call him Uncle out of respect. In our Kurdish culture it's rude just to call someone by their name, you always need a respectful form of address, respected Older Brother, respected Aunt or Uncle – we have special words to show respect. Hussein isn't actually my dad's brother. His father and my grandfather were cousins – but we still call him Uncle Hussein.

The market was in Hussein's house and in it you could find everything you might ever need to live in our village – from shampoo to sweets to school books, kerosene and gas canisters, cigarettes and fabrics, yoghurt and olives.

The market took over one side of his house and crates of fruit and produce were stacked all the way round the outside.

It was a crazy assortment of stuff and only Hussein knew exactly what he had and where it was. He was legendary in the village for his ability to keep track of every item and hold a rigid tab for every man, woman and child customer.

I suppose we should have been glad and grateful for Hussein's ceaseless efforts to cater for all our needs – but his meticulous attention to his business made him miserable company.

He could never greet anyone without including a public reproach for their tab. To my father: "Morning Nuri – it's a lovely day are you off to the river for a spot of fishing? Don't forget you still owe me for the hooks and line you took yesterday…"

To my mother: "Good afternoon Seha – Mashallah don't the girls look lovely today – you haven't forgotten you still owe me for that knicker elastic…"

Or: "Good day Seha – lovely scarf – is it new? It's the colour of pomegranate juice – which reminds me your little Elif helped herself and her sister to a red lolly when they were here with your twins yesterday – I've put

27

it on your slate..."

He'd manage to combine his comments with pleasantries but somehow you always left, feeling a bit told off.

Every family in the village had a tab with Uncle Hussein – us children were often sent on errands by our mothers with lists of supplies and it was common practice for us to call in for refreshments on our way to or from school. The rule was that you showed Uncle Hussein what you had and he would put it on your tab and your dad would settle up every so often.

Back then, when I was five, perhaps because there wasn't a lot to do in the village – or maybe because he was quite annoying – teasing or tricking Uncle Hussein was almost a local sport, certainly among us kids.

The boys spent hours fashioning collections of special tools. Sticks with sharpened points, others with hooks, some with nets. Making and refining tools was a big project for the boys' gang that summer. The excitement of making the tools was as much fun as using them. When they were ready, some of the boys would distract Uncle Hussein, while others climbed the trees to the side of the market and yet more hid behind the low wall at the back.

With Hussein's back turned, boys in the branches would dangle precariously as they attempted to scoop or stab or flick the fruit from the boxes displayed at the front of the market. The stabbing stick proved to be the most successful in skewering apples and oranges and with a flick the stolen spoils could be tossed to the waiting boys behind the wall.

Rarely was the fruit eaten – in fact it was less about stealing than the mission to get one over Uncle Hussein.

And for weeks that summer the joy of their secret success kept nearly every kid in the village delighted.

Of course, it was only a matter of time before Uncle Hussein twigged – and being Hussein he knew how to exact his revenge and seized his chance to make the boys pay.

He found my father and the dads of several other boys enjoying a smoke and a game of backgammon in the overcrowded local tea-room. Uncle Hussein barged through the door carrying two large crates of oranges, which made everyone in the place stop and stare.

Threading his way, with difficulty, between the tables of tea-drinking men, Hussein headed over to my dad and dumped the crates noisily next to his table and said, "Good evening Nuri, Zeyni, gentlemen." He nodded to the group and continued, "I'm sorry to think that you have fallen on hard times, although it would appear that you can still afford tea, tobacco and gaming..." He smiled as he took a moment to survey the detritus of an evening's card playing, tea drinking and smoking – the table littered with empty glasses and overflowing ashtrays. He continued, "But the very idea that your children are sitting at home starving is a cause of great sadness to me.

"That they are reduced to stealing fruit from my market to feed themselves makes me ashamed as a Muslim who has promised to try and help alleviate the suffering of the poor.

"With that end in mind I'm gifting you these crates of oranges to share between your boys – perhaps in future you could persuade them to come into the market, instead of hanging from the branches like monkeys helping themselves. I have plenty of chores that need to be done and will happily reward their hard work with as much fruit as they can eat. Filling their empty bellies and saving their souls at the same time seems a perfect solution to your problem."

Seeing a combination of shame and rage start to spread across the faces of the seated men, Hussein bid them goodnight and scuttled home happy to reflect on a job well-done.

"That'll teach the little buggers," he later told his wife. "I doubt they'll be able to sit down for a week – let alone climb a tree," he smirked. And sure enough the happy gang of fruit thieves soon discovered the error of their ways.

Arriving home that night, carrying a crate of oranges, my happy dad had a face like thunder. "Good evening wife," he said as he greeted my mother, armed with the crate.

"It would appear we have failed as parents," he said, placing the fruit at her feet where she sat, knitting on the verandah. "Did you know," he said, his voice rising as he warmed to his theme. "Did you have any idea that our poor boys are starving? Starving, in fact, for the very fruit that grows here in the beautiful garden you work so hard to tend.

"Starving, despite the fact that they have our permission and blessing to help themselves to ANYTHING," (he was bellowing by now), "on our tab at Hussein's.

"So starving," he spat through gritted teeth at my brothers, who, realising they'd been rumbled, were standing awkwardly in a line in front of the house, "so starving they were reduced to STEALING," he screamed in fury.

Sitting at my mum's feet, holding her knitting wool, I was frozen in shock by my furious father. I'd never seen him angry – let alone so incandescent with rage and shame that actual blobs of spittle were flying out of his mouth as he ranted at my brothers.

And at the word 'STEALING' my horrified mother dropped her knitting needles and clasped her hand over her mouth. "They've stolen from Uncle Hussein? Oh the shame – we'll never live it down. Boys how could you – why would you?" she asked as she turned to give them the most reproachful look.

It was enough to make the younger three, Baran, Bilal and Azad burst into tears. My father continued his theatrical tirade. "Well obviously it's because they're starving and can't get enough oranges to eat. So here you are boys. Here's a whole crate just for you. It's a gift from Hussein." (At the mention of his name the weeping boys started to sob).

"Well come on – what are you waiting for? Tuck in – there must be at least twenty-five each and when you've finished all of those you can go down and do chores for Hussein and he'll reward you with even more."

Knowing better than to argue the boys set to the task of peeling and eating the crate of oranges.

I cried myself to sleep that night – believing that stealing fruit was the very worst crime you could commit. By the morning the boys' fingers and faces were as orange as the fruit and their stomachs as sour.

But none of them has ever stolen since. And looking back I really wish that was the worst crime in the world.

7. THE WARRIORS' RETURN

I was so engrossed in writing and reliving the happiness of life at home that I hadn't realised the time and that it was getting dark and without the sun's warmth, sitting in the courtyard was getting cold and uncomfortable.

But I don't think I would have stopped furiously scribbling in my diary, and feeling the joy that it was bringing me – an emotion I hadn't had for so long – unless I had been interrupted by the return of a wildly elated Rehana.

I could hear them before I saw them – Rehana and the other YPJ girls – singing the Kurdish national anthem in triumphant tone before they burst into the courtyard.

Rehana came straight over to me, with her AK47 slung over her shoulder, and I could tell by her face that she was excited and delighted. Yanking me to my feet she enveloped me in a bear hug before she spoke.

As she released her grip she looked into my eyes and with a smile, said, "They're dead – those filth from this morning." She spat on the floor at the mention of the ratmen.

My legs had gone numb where I'd been sat still for so long. And I wobbled as I realised what she was telling me.

Searching her face for confirmation – I felt a flutter – a little hope that I might not, after all, have to deal with the pain I'd been trying to block out since this morning.

"My mum and the girls?"

"Dilly they weren't there – we haven't found them but we

haven't found their bodies either – so that's something to be glad about. We still have hope…" Her voice trailed off as she didn't have anything other than hope to offer but hope was good.

Hope meant that I could banish the gruesome images from my head – for now anyway. Spying my diary on the floor, Rehana picked it up and flicked through the pages I'd written. "Wow," she said, "you've been really busy." She was clearly impressed and I nodded and held up my claw-like hand as proof of my efforts.

Rehana laughed and slung her arm round my shoulder. "I'm looking forward to reading this," she said passing me the book, "but first we need to eat – I'm starving."

Across the courtyard the other YPJ girls had dumped their weapons with Rojdan who was checking, cleaning and reloading them.

Stripped out of their warrior-wear the girls set to stoking the pit in the open bread oven in the corner of the yard while others produced pans and wood and knives.

Within minutes of their return the five girls, Rehana, Sydrah*, Zosan, Asmin and Songul were sitting in a circle kneading dough for bread and gossiping about their day, as if instead of fighting and killing for their people, they had been shopping at the market. These women were incredible.

I put water on to boil, tied my hair up and joined them as they chatted.

"Seizing the truck was a result," said Sydrah, a tall studious girl from a neighbouring village to mine. I remembered her

* PRONUNCIATION *See-dra*

winning a school prize for reciting large chunks of the Koran.

"What truck?" I asked.

"The airstrikes were targeting the tanks and jeeps that they'd used to break into the east of the city this morning," said Sydrah.

"One truck with a machine gun on the back was pinning us down while providing cover for them to flood into the city. Thank God for the airstrikes. They took out the tanks that were pounding us and as the enemy realised they were sitting ducks for the American planes, they fled the convoys and hid in the streets.

"That made it impossible for the coalition to target them for fear of killing us by mistake. We got the truck and it was loaded with food and crates of guns and ammunition.

"Then we followed the stink of them down into the lower east square and killed them all," she added, very matter-of-factly, as the other girls nodded their approval.

We fell silent for a moment – kneading and shaping the flat bread in stark contrast to the bloodshed and hatred that was shaping our lives.

8. RATS TO the SLAUGHTER

In the ensuing silence we could hear the boys as they arrived outside the courtyard with the prized truck.

Suddenly the door in the wall burst open and they poured in – seventeen of them in total, a YPG patrol of eleven and the six other girls from Rehana's YPJ patrol. They were laden with sacks and crates seized from the stolen truck.

Like the girls, they were in very high spirits – and it was tangible that all hopes and fears of everyone in this courtyard hung on the destruction of the ratmen. Their death was a cause to celebrate – from this morning when they came at us out of the night, taking us by surprise with their strength in spitefulness and in numbers and weapons and even tanks – to now when they've been forced back out of the city – several tanks destroyed and many of them dead in our streets.

The airstrikes and the fighting had lasted all day – it had provided a rattling chorus while I was writing. At first, sharp and distracting in the streets nearby, then interrupted by an airstrike. Then hours of battling by the lower square and slowly the sounds diminished as the ratmen faced with failure and death, scurried back to the holes they had crawled out from.

Now it was time to celebrate the bravery and success of the day. The YPG team and half of the YPJ women had been distributing the spoils to our friends around the city as Rehana and the other girls returned to make bread.

When they came back, they handed the food that was left to

the little group of cooks. There were eggs and cheese, tomatoes, olives and cucumber, fresh yoghurt, honey and even jam.

The boys spread a blanket on the floor, boiled the eggs and cut and washed the salty village cheese, while I helped cut tomatoes and cucumber. Within minutes of their arrival we were all sat, cross-legged round the blanket tucking in to warm bread with cheese and eggs and watermelon washed down with a glass of sweet tea. The food helped settle the odd, sick feeling I'd had all day and after we'd all cleared up and made fresh tea we settled back into a circle to talk through the events of the day.

As one of the most senior and experienced fighters among us, Rehana spoke first. "Today was a good day," she began. "Good 'cos we're all still here and we're not hungry," she beamed round the group.

Smiling back at her, Sydrah swallowed hard and fighting back tears she tried to speak without crying. "Yes we are all here – but for a moment today I was expecting to die…"

"Me too," nodded Asmin.

"You saved our lives Rehana – AGAIN…" they choroused.

"You are most welcome – it was my pleasure," laughed Rehana making a mock bow.

"That was some shooting, Rehana," complimented Abdullah – the leader of the boys' patrol. "When the Bixi machine gun

jammed I thought we were all done for – thank God for you…"
he added.

Watching the smile on Rehana's face, I realised how pleased
and proud she was at the comments from her friends.

"What happened? Tell me – please," I begged, desperate to
hear of payback, revenge, some sign that that we had a chance
to take back control.

"I'll tell you what happened," said Asmin. "Me, Sydrah
and Songul walked straight into the lion's den – that's what
happened," she said, turning to me and pulling a funny face.

"Go on – then what?" I implored. "Tell me, don't tease me."

"Well we were checking through the streets after the airstrike.
We knew there were many straggling scumbags hiding from
the drones and satellite cameras.

"We were clearing house by house, street by street. But as
we fought our way into the lower square we stopped to check
our ammo. Sydrah leant against a wall and it just collapsed.
The whole thing just fell over in one piece and there on the other
side, not more than five metres from us was an entire enemy
patrol. For a moment we all just stared at each other. There were
eighteen of them – facing us. Neither me, nor Songul had any
ammunition left and Sydrah and Zosan were almost out.

"I don't know who was more surprised, them or us – but
we were seriously outnumbered and as I saw that revolting smirk
spread between them I was sure we were dead.

"Why? Why do they smirk like that about killing people?
Why does it bring them so much pleasure?" Asmin wondered
out loud – but as no one had an answer for her, she continued.
"Standing facing them in that square can only have been a
couple of seconds but it felt like forever. No one wanted to make
the first move. Then suddenly the smirks seemed to slide off
their faces and one by one they hit the floor – I didn't even hear

the bullets.

"None of them could see where the attack was coming from and we had no idea either but within a blink, six of them were dead on the floor by my feet.

"I could hear you lot screaming to Abdullah," she said nodding towards her comrades, "but they were still dropping like flies.

"The chaos snapped us out of our trance and Sydrah and Zosan managed to take out a couple. It was over in seconds and when they were all dead in the dust we heard a wolf-whistle from way above our heads and Rehana's smiling face waving from the top floor of a house at the back of the square. I don't know who was more delighted," Asmin smiled across at Rehana.

"How did you get up there so fast?" she asked.

"When we split up to enter the square from different sides I could hear them talking but I could neither see them nor warn you without alerting them," said Rehana.

"I realised they were near us somewhere in the rubble – instead of crossing the square I doubled back and ran to the top of that building. From the top window I could see you walking straight towards them. I radioed Abdullah but the Bixi was jammed – so that just left me.

"I had them in my sights just as you brought the wall down – the looks on your faces – it was a picture," laughed Rehana.

"Anyway it was my fear that I'd miss them and hit you instead – that's why I hesitated. But you are right Asmin – when I saw that smirk spread among them I knew you only had moments left – I also knew that you'd rather die from my bullet than their blade."

Sydrah, Asmin, Songul and Zosan all nodded their agreement. That was a no-brainer. "I picked off the first three on the edge of the group and when I knew I was good for distance and wind speed I just ploughed on through the rest." Her trademark grin spread across her face.

Ercan*, a studious boy with glasses, chipped in, "That's better than good Reh. That's easily a distance of 400 metres – there's not many who could make a target from there."

Extracting a grubby pocket notebook he began to jot things with a stubby little pencil before suddenly exclaiming, "Hey Reh – saving the girls in the square today takes your tally of terrorists to over one hundred you've killed alone – that could be the record for a lone sniper… You could be famous," he smiled before adding shyly, "When this is all over will you teach me to shoot like that?"

"Better for all of us if you could learn now," joked Abdullah as he slapped Ercan on the back. "So you reckon Rehana is the best shot ever?" he taunted.

"What's my tally, Ercan?"

"Yours is up there Abdullah – but you've been using the Bixi and the M16 – Reh has just got that old rifle."

* PRONUNCIATION *Air-jan*

"Yeah it might be old but at least she's got bullets for it," snapped Zosan.

"You should be glad it was her with the bullets," Asmin replied. "You couldn't have hit them standing right in front of you – you're shocking…"

Joking and boasting, bragging and teasing – it was a big part of our culture and the conversation batted backwards and forwards between us as a small group sorted through phones and papers they'd taken from the dead men. Touching and smelling their foul possessions revolted me but Ercan quickly explained the importance of trawling through their phones.

"We glean as much intelligence as we can from their phones and share a lot of it with the Americans," he explained.

"Their recently dialled numbers tell us who they're in contact with and they can be tracked and followed with GPS. Also they share messages and emails which give us a better insight into their thinking. They're avid photographers and record in great detail a lot of their executions – these they share on the internet. Apparently they use it as propaganda to attract other sickos from around the world to come and join them," Ercan explained.

"You're kidding me," I was stunned. "Seriously? Normal people have seen what the ratmen are doing and thought 'beheading and barbarism – that's right up my street' and actually travelled across the world to join them?" I could not believe what Ercan was telling me – this was the destruction of Syria.

"Yeah I know, incredible isn't it?" muttered Ercan as he continued to skim through a pile of mobile phones in front of him.

"The English are the worst. Hundreds of them have oiled their way over here. They're brown skinned but British. They reckon they're Muslims but they love themselves more than God. Physically they're weak and mentally they're weird. We reckon it's to cover up their inability to fight or shoot that they come up with the sickest forms of torture.

"It was a group of British and Tunisian boys that came to my village. Most people had already fled – those left were killed or sold as slaves. We only know what happened from the one child that survived – he hid in a water butt and that's what saved him. They used shepherd dogs to round up the remainder – they took the women and then set the dogs on the kids."

"Shepherd dogs – Kangals?" I questioned in disbelief. "They turned on kids?"

I thought of our own gentle, protective pack of dogs.

"They're starved and beaten – you can't really blame them," said Ercan – and although I was completely fascinated by what he was telling me I found I was suddenly distracted by an image that flickered across the screen of the phone he was holding.

I only caught a glimpse out of the corner of my eye – but it was unmistakable, and my stomach lurched.

"Stop – Ercan, what was that? Go back. Please – please…"

I recognised it instantly – the pretty pink rose pattern – it was Hira's dress. It was her favourite, not that she had many, but she loved the pink one for its patch pockets and matching knickers. She loved filling the pockets with mud and worms and sweets and suddenly there she was filling the screen of the telephone, just as I had last seen her, terrified, sobbing, being pinned to the floor, a blade at her throat.

Tears were streaming down my face and

splashing onto the screen that I had snatched from Ercan's hand.

Ercan squeezed my shoulders. "Is that your sister?" he asked peering at the snap.

I nodded – unable to speak.

"Ok well there's things we can find out from this phone," said Ercan gently prising it from my fingers.

"Give me a minute and I'll see what I can do."

"Promise you'll tell me the truth Ercan," I begged him, catching hold of his arm. "Good or bad – promise me."

Holding my gaze he said, "I promise Dilly – I understand – I've got little sisters too remember?" I nodded and let go of his arm.

9. VISITORS and Hope

I wandered back to the pomegranate tree and thought about writing some more of my diary but I didn't have the heart.

Songul was singing a folk song while the others were checking and cleaning equipment for the next day.

Her voice was clear and reedy as she sang the lament – it was one of my mother's favourites and one that I knew well and almost without thinking I joined with Songul, singing the harmonies, remembering happier times, until we were interrupted by crackling messages coming through on the radio.

Suddenly everyone was on their feet and racing to tidy up. "What is it? What's happening Reh?" I asked as she raced to fasten her jacket and shoulder her gun.

"Our commander's coming, General Zinar – and he's bringing some important visitors – they want to take a look at that crate of guns we took from the truck," she explained. "They want to find out who's supplying them."

As she spoke the door in the wall opened and a group of men – important looking men – walked in. There were ten of them, six were Kurdish commanders, Syrian YPG and Iraqi Peshmerga, and although the other four were clearly soldiers they looked very different.

Their combats were lighter and so was their skin and hair. As the leaders of their patrols, Rehana and Abdullah were already greeting the guests. The other twenty-two soldiers – including the two injured boys who had struggled to their feet

– were standing to attention in two straight lines, ready for inspection. YPJ girls on one side and the YPG unit on the other.

Not sure what I was supposed to do, I joined on the end of the YPJ line and stood up straight. As the visitors made their way into the courtyard, Rehana and Abdullah took it in turns to introduce each member of their unit.

And with each little introduction I learned more about the bravery and sacrifice of each of them.

It was oddly comforting to realise that every one of us in the courtyard had lost someone they loved at the hands of the ratmen.

As the officers made their way towards me I was secretly hoping that they might mistake me for one of the patrol and I could stay. It was what I wanted more than anything. But glancing down at my feet I realised that I was wearing my brother's boots tied up with blue nylon string, and my old khaki jeans were so short that where they flared out at the bottom, they didn't even reach the top of the boots. My grubby white T-shirt and big belt completed my outfit. It was the same thing I'd been wearing for months now – ever since we fled Rojava for the safety of Lanaco and clearly not the uniform of a soldier.

"And who do we have here, Rehana?" questioned one of

the officers. "You starting a new junior wing of the YPJ?" he continued. He was smiling as he spoke, his eyes twinkling as he waited for a response.

But it was Abdullah who cut in with the answer. "This is Dilvan – General – Dilvan Haco*," he seemed to lay heavy emphasis on my surname and for a moment I was confused. "Haco?" questioned the officer, spinning round to Abdullah who was smiling and nodding at him.

"You any relation to Nuri Haco, girl?" he demanded.

Nodding I stuttered in surprise as I answered, "My dad and my brother…"

"He's your dad and your brother?" boomed the officer.

"No, Sir, both my dad and my brother are called Nuri Haco – my dad's a lot older than my brother and…"

Wreathed in smiles the officer leant towards me and smothered me in a bear hug – squeezing me and lifting me off my feet. His beard tickled my chin as he kissed me on both cheeks before setting me back on the ground.

"Wyyy Masallah! Dilvan Haco!" he exclaimed before pulling me into another bear hug. "Look at you – just look at you – how could I not have known – you have your dad's eyes," he smiled down at me, ruffling my hair.

"Me and your dad go way back, Dilvan. We trained and fought together over twenty years ago – back in the first Gulf War – together we helped to shape the first free Kurdistan," he roared, punching the air in victory.

"Azadiya Kurdistan," chanted all of us in joyful response.

"Your dad's a good man – one of the best – we lost touch over the years but we were reunited three months ago when he arrived on Mount Tilsakan with your brothers.

* PRONUNCIATION *Ha-jo*

45

"Hey Jake, Richard," he called out to the fair soldiers – gesturing for them to come over.

As they approached, General Zinar told me they were American officers – here to help us and to help organise the coalition strategy.

Using one of the other Kurdish officers as a translator, the general quickly explained who I was, and after a delay while his words were repeated in English – I was suddenly the centre of all the attention.

Everyone was talking at once – mainly telling each other how great my dad was. I was so delighted just to hear his name that it took me a moment before I had a chance to ask, "Are they all OK? Are they coming back?"

"They're better than OK – they're brilliant," replied General Zinar. What they did on Tilsakan was unbelievable. They're heroes – you should be really proud of them Dilvan.

"They're on their way here right now. We only beat them because we got a lift with these kind Americans in their helicopter – but I'm expecting them all here in the next couple of days – so all we need to do is keep you safe and we'll have one hell of a reunion when they arrive. How's your mum and sisters?"

The mention of my mum and sisters wiped the smile off my face in a second and the general, seeing my distress, looked to Rehana.

"This morning, Sir," she explained, "when the enemy came at us – the family were in the lower east side of the city. Dilvan was out searching for food thank God. We came across her as we raced down to confront them.

"We saw them take her mum and her sister Elif. The baby was… well we don't exactly know what's happened to the baby, Sir," she said, grimacing and raising her palms in a gesture of despair.

"Excuse me for interrupting Sir – but I think we just got an idea of what happened to Dilly's sister this morning in that square," interrupted Ercan.

"We found an image of Hira on one of their phones. I was just trawling through it to see if we could find anything more – if we could discover what might have happened to her." As he was talking he'd produced the phone and scrolled through hundreds of images of bodies and grinning goons with big guns and of people being beheaded and on and on his thumb flicked across the screen until they reached Hira.

Handing the phone to the general, Ercan continued, "The first thing you realise is you don't see her beheaded. All the other images and clips end with them grinning as they hold the head aloft by its hair. But not Hira." He was very matter-of-fact as he spoke but his quiet words conjured horrible images in my head… I gritted my teeth, swallowed and exhaled sharply forcing myself to continue listening to Hira's fate… but I was struggling. Images of Hira sitting on my lap, her squishy baby cheeks and rosebud lips contorting as she aped the funny faces I was pulling, giggling and trying to force her chubby, usually sticky, fingers in my mouth. Just hearing Ercan say her name made me long for her… hurt for her physically. My stomach now seemed to make an almighty leap into my throat and I thought I might be sick on the general's shoes.

I realised Ercan had stopped talking and everyone was looking at me. I tried to speak but my mouth kind of crumpled so I just shrugged and stared at the blue string on my boots as Ercan continued.

"What's possibly even more important is that this is the only image of Hira. In fact the shots straight after this on the phone camera are just a blurry image of the sky. There's plumes of black smoke obscuring part of the frame."

General Zinar took the phone and peered closely at it through his glasses. I found myself staring at him as he studied the picture – with his greying hair and square jaw he reminded me of my dad.

"The fact they didn't record the whole gruesome event is a good sign. And also Hira is in one of a burst of three photos: the one of her, then two shots of the smoke filled sky – taken at 07.59 – the airstrike was at 08.00 hours.

"We've been back to the square and there's no baby's body there – I know they like to collect the heads as souvenirs but they generally leave the bodies where they fall." Ercan was racing to make his point but from the look on the general's face, he was clearly way ahead of him, whereas I was struggling to fan the little flicker of hope that I felt stirring.

"What EXACTLY are you saying, Ercan?" I demanded. "I can't be EXACT," he stressed. "I'm guessing but it's an educated guess that whoever was taking the pictures was blown off their feet by the airstrike, dropping the phone, and although that doesn't tell us what happened to Hira, we are fairly certain that they didn't have time to stop and execute people in the middle of an airstrike. Who knows what might have happened to her in the chaos?"

Everyone fell silent as the Americans looked at the pictures. Rehana reached out her hand for mine. "It's like I said, Dilly," she whispered to me, "there's still hope." She squeezed my hand as one of the Americans let out a low whistle under his breath.

I didn't understand the words he used but I got the sense of it as he spat on the floor. The translator soon updated them on Hira and I heard my dad and brothers' names being mentioned as the men looked at me, nodding and talking among themselves.

The translator, a Turkish Kurd named Ali, spoke very good English. He later told me he'd learnt English working as a barman in the tourist resorts. He'd left his own bar business to join the fight for Lanaco a few weeks before and although I was glad to see him I wasn't surprised – Kurds stick together.

The translator shook my hand and introduced himself. "I'm Ali. I'm pleased to meet you and sorry about your sister. I'm working with the Americans and they'd like to talk to you for a moment – if that's OK?" he asked.

Two of the Americans were looking at the rifles in the crate – the other two were sitting on plastic chairs and spooning sugar into black tea as I walked over to them.

Ali introduced them as Jake and Richard and we all smiled at each other. Through Ali we managed to talk for a while. Richard, the older one told me he had daughters of the same ages as Hira and me. He said he was very sad to see the picture of Hira but it reminded him why he was here – so far from his own children.

Richard said he was going to ask his colleagues in America for all the satellite pictures taken at the time of the airstrike to see if there were any more images of Hira or the truck that took my mum and Elif.

I thought it was a brilliant idea and he went off with Ali to ask Ercan for the photos – leaving me sitting, drinking tea, with the other American, Jake.

"Do you speak English?? Eeennnggglliiiiiiiissshhhhhh?"

he repeatedly, loudly and slowly.

"Hay–lo mi nim is Dilvan," I replied.

"I am turteen yurs awld… wan, too, tree, for, five…" I said, racking my brains for more.

He smiled, realising my schoolgirl English wasn't up to a conversation and opted for sign language instead.

"You," he said pointing at me.

"You, brother (for this he raised his hand above my head) good," he smiled and gave a thumbs up.

I smiled back politely but not really understanding. Seeing the obvious confusion on my face, Jake produced his phone and took a moment to find a picture. Handing it to me I saw Jake, on a mountain in a group of Peshmerga. The down-draught from a helicopter in the background was making them duck and hold onto their caps – but they'd stopped to take a snap – smiling, arms round each other's shoulders, thumbs up and as I looked more closely I realised that, standing next to Jake, smiling back at me, was my brother Nuri.

Several hours later – after I'd made Ali squeeze every drop of information about my brothers from Jake I was finally exhausted.

Lying under a horsehair blanket on a mattress in the courtyard, snuggled between Rehana and Sydrah for warmth, I tried to recap on the events of that day. There were so many – and so many important ones – that I struggled to recall them in order and realised that I had a lot to write in my diary in the morning. But as I drifted into sleep the glimpse of my brother's smiling face and the knowledge that he and the others were safe, made my heart soar.

10. ... and so it Begins...

We were up with the sun and straight to chores. Ercan had already started cutting up watermelon and washing more salty cheese for breakfast.

Rehana, I knew, was itching to get a look at the rifles taken the day before and I was keen to write about everything that had happened since I'd put my diary down early yesterday evening.

Pinching a slice of watermelon from Ercan, I popped it in my mouth and sucked the juice from my fingers before opening my diary for the second day and starting to write.

11th October 2014

Yesterday I lost my mother and sisters, but they may not be lost forever and I may have found my father and brothers... But they weren't lost, exactly.

Things had been changing in Syria for some time – there'd been a civil war between the Syrian people and the president for several years – but, until recently, events hadn't reached us.

Like I said before, although we were in Syria, we Kurds pretty much looked after ourselves separately to the rest of the country. And although we really didn't like President Assad we'd reached a kind of agreement that we would leave him alone if he left us alone.

The sudden surge of a black plague across Iraq last year, seemed to happen while we were looking the other way. It took many of us by surprise I think.

I remember the men in our village meeting and talking and planning in the village room – the feeling of fear spreading at reports of their atrocities and rapid success in storming across Iraq – virtually unopposed by the Iraqi army.

My dad had been away to war in the past and watching the stain of the enemy spread ever closer he and my brothers knew that it was just a matter of time before they would have to pick up weapons and defend our home once again.

In fact it was before the killer cult reached us way up on Syria's northern border, that my dad, who could stand it no longer, took my brothers and their guns and went to fight.

Together we'd watched as thousands of terrified people fled into Iraqi Kurdistan for protection from the terrorists' death squads.

We watched world news reports showing convoys of ratmen rolling across Iraq. They were stopping traffic and pulling people out of cars. They shot one man because he looked like a teacher. By the end of the report my mum was in tears and my dad looked very angry. But it was the plight of the Yazidis on Mount Tilsakan that was the final straw for him.

The ratmen appear to believe that they are like God and have the power of life and death over the rest of us. Their leader, a short fat man I call the ratdaddy – decided that all of the Yazidis, an ancient Christian tribe, should die and to that end he had sent his ratmen to kill them.

The news reporter, a woman, struggled not to cry as she gave her shocking account. "Thousands of Yazidis in the Kurdish region of Iraq remain stranded with nowhere to go," she said.

"Human rights groups are examining claims of genocide by terrorist groups against the Yazidi religious minority in Iraq…" The reporter spoke to a few survivors of an attack – one fifteen-year-old boy told how he'd seen five of his brothers and his dad shot – he'd managed to survive by hiding under the dead bodies.

The report revealed that from a town of 1,800 people less than 200 Yazidis had survived the attack.

Watching these hopeless, helpless people, fleeing from certain death was the limit for my dad. Calling my brothers together he told them, "While we sit here the Yazidis are being wiped out. Our Kurdish cousins in Iraq are being overwhelmed. I cannot stand by for another day and watch this brutality. I think we should go and stand with them and hope others do the same."

And so it was decided that my dad and brothers and some of my uncles and cousins would travel together through Turkey to reach Iraq and join their cousins there and see what help they could offer to the Yazidis.

We all cried as they left – I remember me and my mum and the girls standing out on the track waving them off. Elif was trying to be brave, trying not to cry – but Hira was furious watching her legion of adoring fans leaving. My dad kissed her little fat face for the last time and passed her to my mum and as she realised that they were leaving without her, she flung back her head and screamed in fury trying to fight her way out of my mum's arms and chase after them. But when they disappeared out of sight her fury gave way to misery and she threw herself onto the dirt and sobbed.

Hitching her up onto her hip, my mum, said, "Well that's that. Peace and quiet and no smelly socks for a while!" She was trying to cheer us up. I smiled and Elif giggled.

"That's the spirit – we've no time for tears now – we've got all the work to do," she laughed at the look of horror on Elif's face. "It's all right – we don't have to start straight away," she soothed. "Let's go down to the market and get an ice-lolly to cheer this baby up," she said flinging Hira up in the air and catching her.

"Lolly lolly," laughed the baby – completely recovered from her

sobbing fit just minutes earlier and even Elif looked delighted at
the prospect.

For me it was going to take more than a lolly to shake the feeling
of dread that was threatening to reduce me to a sobbing heap on
the floor.

"If it's OK with you I've got some homework to finish Mum and
I want to check on the puppies..."

My mum took my chin in her hand and inspected me closely.

"As long as you're not going to sit and sob, Dilly?" she questioned,
searching my face for reassurance.

I mustered a weak smile and shrugged. What difference would
crying make? Tears weren't going to stop terrorists.

Hugging me to her, my mum kissed my forehead and whispered
into my hair, "I love you sweetheart. Be strong. We have to for Hira
and Elif."

I nodded my agreement and smiled as I watched them wander
towards the market before turning and dashing back up the track.
I ran through the orchard of fruit trees at the side of the house and
round to the back where the ground drops away to the river and you
have an unspoilt view across the valley up to Turkey on my left and

out across the Syrian plains in front of me
and to my right.

I knew that I would get a glimpse of
my dad and the little convoy of cars as they
headed to the Turkish border and I desperately
felt the need to send them my love and
pray urgently for their safe return.

But as I skidded to a halt I was surprised
to see Rehana already standing there, with
her back to me, staring out across the valley.
Spinning round in surprise I saw she had tears
streaming down her face.

55

There was no need for explanations, she loved my brother Nuri as much as I did and I'd known it would be hard for her to see him go. Seeing her face contorted in misery tipped me over the edge, and ignoring my mum's words, we hugged each other and sobbed.

"I did really try not to cry," she sobbed. "I know how much Nuri hates tears – I managed to be really cheerful when we said goodbye – but now he's gone and it feels like he's taken my strength with him."

"I just wanted to wave one last time and send them my love..." I trailed off as, right on cue, the little convoy of cars appeared in the distance and started wending its way towards Turkey. We stood watching in silence for a moment, holding hands, sending our love and prayers, tears streaming down our faces.

Rehana brushed away her tears as I sniffed. "Look at you – snot face," she laughed. "Nuri would be soooo proud!" I didn't reply – just widened my gaze in reproach at her swollen tear-stained face and red eyes.

Stung by the slight, Rehana nodded, "Come on Dilly, we can do better than this, let's send them off with some pride."

And standing to attention she raised her right hand in the victory salute and started to sing our Kurdish national anthem. Raising my hand the same, we sang together at the tops of our voices hoping it would carry on the wind to our loved ones...

"Oh, enemy! The Kurdish people live on,
They have not been crushed by the weapons of any time
Let no one say Kurds are dead, they are living
They live and never shall we lower our flag."

We had hardly finished the first verse before a little gang of neighbours' kids and cousins peered round the back of our house to see who was singing.

Seeing me and Rehana standing, saluting, singing our hearts out

across the valley to a disappearing convoy of cars – they needed
no further explanation or, indeed, invitation. Suddenly our ranks were
swelled to eight, then twelve as some of the boys ran up to join in.
There were nineteen of us for the second verse.

"We are descendants of the red banner of the revolution
Look at our past, how bloody it is
Let no one say Kurds are dead,
They are living,
They live and never shall we lower our flag."

By the end of the second verse, the straggly line of singing kids
ranged across the cliff top. Even the Kangals, sensing the emotion,
strained to see what the fuss was about as we sang on...

"The Kurdish youth rise bravely,
With their blood they coloured the crown of life
Let no one say Kurds are dead, they are living
They live and never shall we lower our flag."

I swear by now every child in the village and many of the adults
too had joined their voices to our makeshift choir – willing the
wind to carry our message of love and determination and pride
across the river, across the valley...

"We are the descendants of the Medes and Cyaxares
Stan is our religion, our credo,
Let no one say Kurds are dead, they are living
They live and never shall we lower our flag."

And then, as we watched, the little convoy slowed, then
stopped. We could see the line of car doors opening and there

they were. My dad and brothers and cousins lined up across the valley, arms raised in salute, singing back to us, united we sang together across the plains. All of us smiling now – my heart soaring with love and pride, goosebumps prickling my arms as we sang on...

"The Kurdish youth are ready, it is prepared
To give their life as the supreme sacrifice
Let no one say Kurds are dead, they are living
They live and never shall we lower our flag."

I'm sure that many of the kids believed our voices alone brought the convoy to a standstill – turns out it was my aunt who called my dad on his phone in the car so they could hear us singing. But no matter how it happened it will be a moment I'll never forget.

When the last echoes had faded Rehana turned to me beaming and said, "Now that was a send-off to be proud of!"

11. SURVIVORS OF TILSAKAN

That was three months ago and that was the last time I saw my father and brothers – until last night when Jake showed me the photo of Nuri and told me how they had helped to save the last living Yazidis – the only remaining survivors of that ancient tribe.

After we'd waved and sung them off – they had travelled on through Turkey and into Iraqi Kurdistan where they were overwhelmed by the chaos and misery they discovered at the end of their long drive.

Through Ali, Jake described the plight of the thousands of desperate refugees who had flooded into Kurdistan for protection from the ratmen. Starving, homeless and often shoeless these people were living on the streets – but for the time being they were safe and my father passed on to the Kurdish border with Iraq and into territory now claimed by the caliphate.

For several weeks before their departure and on their journey, my father had been in contact with his old Kurdish comrades – including General Zinar – who was ready and waiting for him when he reached the border.

According to Jake, the Kurdish warriors were tasked with preventing the ratmen from reaching the top of Mount Tilsakan – where hundreds of Yazidis had fled and were now trapped.

He told me that my twin brothers, Baran and Bilal, had become legends of the rescue. They had taken up a position halfway up the mountain – overlooking the advance of the ratmen.

For three days – without reinforcements – they picked off scores of the greasy-haired swarm – including the son and nephew of one of the terrorists' richest supporters from Saudi Arabia.

Jake said American intelligence listened in to conversations between the terrorists. He said the commanders were screaming in fury and embarrassment at the death of the Arab boys. Apparently their oil-rich benefactor had been given assurances about their safety by the ratdaddy himself. Jake said the boys wanted to have a 'jihadi gap-year' – a year out of studying to enjoy a bit of beheading and murder. They'd been promised an easy couple of weeks executing unarmed Yazidis and absolutely no harm was supposed to come to them.

So you can imagine how very cross the rich man must have been when my brothers shot them both dead.

While my brothers and others slowed the ratmen, my dad and Nuri, Sela and Azad continued to the very top of the mountain leading straggling Yazidis – including an old man Azad carried on his back.

It was hard to take in everything Jake had told me. I felt like I was just getting snippets – little glimpses of what had happened. But probably because he was talking through an interpreter he tried to keep it simple.

He told me that my dad had delivered a baby in a cave and the grateful mother had called the baby Haco – in honour of the man who had stayed to protect and help her.

Jake's role was flying one of the helicopters that waited for my dad to secure the mountain top before they could swoop down and pluck the Yazidis to safety.

The plight of the people on the mountain had clearly upset Jake – they had fled their homes in fear for their lives and many had been stranded on the mountain, with no food or water for days. They had no shade or shelter from the sun – and as it was mid-August – the sun was fierce.

But the hardest part for Jake to tell was the end of his story – once they had cleared a safe landing for the helicopters.

They worked together all day – ferrying the sick and the elderly, the women and the children and then the rest of the men. "We only had the two choppers – it's all we had," Jake kept explaining to me.

It was deemed too dangerous to fly after dark and so on the final trip of the day Jake loaded all the remaining Yazidis along with the Kurds who'd helped them, including my family, onto his helicopter.

He apologised as he told me that he tried his best but the helicopter wouldn't take off. It was too heavy and of course it was my dad, followed by my brothers who volunteered to get off.

I think he felt very guilty about having to leave them behind. He looked sad, maybe embarrassed as he told me that they'd shaken his hand and thanked him for all his help.

He promised he'd return for them at first light – but by the morning the enemy had overrun the mountain top after realising the Kurds had pulled out. Jake couldn't return to the mountain and until yesterday had no idea what had happened to my dad and brothers.

He said he was ashamed to face me and tell me what had happened – he said that leaving men behind was unforgivable.

It was a difficult conversation and not one that I was used to – Kurdish men rarely say sorry and never admit to making mistakes.

"My dad," I told him, "would be perfectly horrified to think he needed rescuing.

"He and my brothers went to help the Yazidis – without your helicopter they would all have died right there on that mountain. You shouldn't be ashamed. You should be proud of yourself. You picked the right side and you helped. If everybody did that there would be no black plague – they would be finished already. That's what my dad would say if he were here."

Jake seemed relieved – more so after he'd learnt from General

Zinar that my dad and brothers had scaled down the north face of the mountain using ropes he'd left them and arrived back safely behind Kurdish lines within a couple of days.

What hadn't made sense to me, was why they hadn't returned home. They would have known of the siege at Lanaco and what that meant for us. If they weren't dead I couldn't understand why they weren't here.

Until last night that was. Then the general explained that as they re-entered Turkey they were arrested and thrown in jail as suspected Kurdish terrorists.

The Turks have hated us for years – frightened that one day we Kurds will all join together and make our own big country out of the parts of Syria, Iraq and Turkey where we live. And the bit of Turkey where we live is the bit that has all the oil.

Just learning that my dad and brothers were all safe and away from the fighting was a big deal and sent me to sleep, hopeful.

12. Saving Myself

By this morning the reality of my situation had sunk in a little further. Without my mum and sisters and with no idea when my dad and brothers might be released by the Turks, it had become clear that anything that was to be done for my family was going to have to be done by me.

Only a short while ago I was at my aunties' house with my mum and my sisters. I was a daughter, a niece, a big-sister – now I was the lone survivor of my entire family. But with the luck of the pomegranate tree, I intended to be their saviour. The misery and desperation I had felt yesterday had passed and been replaced with a new determination.

The Americans were preparing to leave so I stopped writing and went to say goodbye to my new friend Jake.

Dragging Ali with me to translate I took the chance to ask if they had any more pictures or information about my mum and sisters.

"Richard has requested all the satellite images from that position," said Jake. "It shouldn't take long for them to be sent through."

"Yes, great but you're leaving – how will I reach you – how will I know?" I asked.

Jake took my diary from my hand and on the inside of the

back cover he wrote his email address and phone number for me. He smiled as he handed it back and then paused, realising his mistake. "You don't have a phone do you Dilly?" he said.

As I shook my head, Ali offered a solution. He and Jake swapped numbers and Jake promised to forward anything to Ali who would pass it to Rehana or Ercan to get to me. Satisfied that we had a plan I smiled and hugged Jake. In less than a day he'd gone from foreign stranger to family friend and I knew that he wouldn't let me down. I knew it was the chance he wanted, to make amends for leaving my dad and brothers on that mountain.

JAKE

jake1721@westwo.sy

001-35649 886

Saying goodbye to that link with them was hard – but I was confident that Jake would do everything in his power to help me reunite the remnants of my family.

Before they left, the Americans had delighted Rehana by showing her the complicated intricacies involved in firing one of the laser-guided rifles.

Handing her one to keep, General Zinar said, "I heard about your shooting yesterday, Rehana – not sure you actually need one of these," he teased.

But for once Rehana was silent – speechless with wonder as she gazed at the gun.

"Take it, take Dilvan to safety and take a couple of days' break – you've earnt it," smiled the general.

"Sir," I interrupted. "Sir, couldn't I stay – please? I'd help and…" But the general raised his hand to silence my pleas.

Cupping my chin in his palm, he stroked my cheek with his thumb and smiled.

"Hey Dilvan, I'm not taking any chances with your safety, sweetheart. I'm an old soldier and there's not much that scares me – but I wouldn't want to get on the wrong side of your father. I need to keep you safe until he gets back and Lanaco is not the safest place to be right now.

"We're expecting an onslaught in the next few days…"

"Yes, that's why I should stay and help – you'll need all the help you can get…" He paused for a moment but I realised it was hopeless as I saw the smile fade on his face.

"Look Dilvan, I know you want to help. But right now the best way you can help is by staying safe.

"Between them, your dad and brothers have managed to infuriate the miscreants that run that shambles – you should know that they would relish the opportunity to make an example of you – you need to keep your head down and firmly attached to your shoulders and I can't guarantee that'll be possible in Lanaco.

"Go with Rehana across the border to safety. I promise to personally reunite you with your dad once he's released. OK?"

I nodded – there wasn't much else I could do – he was right and he was a general and everyone in this courtyard would do exactly as he said.

We were interrupted by the arrival of some of the Lanaco militia. These were old men, too old for the ranks of the YPG – but just as determined to stay and fight – with their white whiskers and bent backs it was a 'grandad's army' that tottered into the courtyard in search of extra ammunition.

General Zinar smiled and nodded at me before he was called back to the work of war.

The Americans had gone, the general was leaving, the courtyard was busy with packing and back-slapping and farewells. It felt like we'd been saying goodbye continuously for the last few months. I now recognised the false brightness in people's eyes and voices – masking the fear and misery.

I decided to escape, momentarily, by diving back into my diary. I plucked a pomegranate from the tree and broke it open. Using my nail I flicked a few of the ruby seeds onto my finger and popped them in my mouth as I slid my back down the wall in a quiet corner and started writing again.

13. FAREWELL to ROJAVA

So I was now to leave Lanaco. It was only a couple of months ago that we'd left the village. In fact it was very shortly after my dad and the boys had gone to Iraq. And at that time we hadn't seen it coming so fast. All the news reports of the fighting were coming from northern Iraq – Mosul had fallen and people expected the ratmen to sweep down to the capital – Baghdad – but they surprised everyone by suddenly turning north-west and heading straight for us.

The YPG had sent patrols to all the outlying villages – warning everyone that the black stain of the caliphate would soon engulf us. Running home from school I could feel the panic spread through the village. Women were sobbing as they packed and worried men huddled in groups making plans or shouting orders to each other.

Reaching our house, I found my mum surprisingly calm – waiting for me on the verandah with a glass of tea.

"You've heard already?" she said as I walked across the garden. I nodded as she continued. "We're going to have to walk to Lanaco, with the girls and whatever else we can carry, Dilly. It's not going to be much – but hopefully it won't be forever," she smiled.

"I've packed already," she gestured to a sports bag, my dad's old army rucksack and a big holdall bulging with our belongings.

Taking my hand she wrapped it round her waist and we wandered into the garden.

I knew my mum was saying goodbye to the fruit trees she'd raised with love over many years. We had lemons and dates and persimmon,

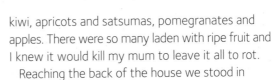

kiwi, apricots and satsumas, pomegranates and apples. There were so many laden with ripe fruit and I knew it would kill my mum to leave it all to rot.

Reaching the back of the house we stood in silence for a moment looking down towards the river. Then hugging me closer she said, "You know we can't take the dogs, Dilly. It's just impossible." And her gentle words brought a new misery into my life.

I don't know why it hadn't occurred to me sooner.

The dogs, descendants of the great Xabur that had first united my parents, had always been part of our family.

Currently there were seven in the pack. There was Xabur (grandson of the original and a chip off the old block), his partner Xena and five of their puppies. It was the puppies that had kept me and my sisters happy since my dad left. They were well over a year old and should all have gone as shepherding dogs by now – but with all the upheaval in the country there were few farmers left and so they had stayed with us – much to our delight. They were the best fun EVER. There were enough of them that we could harness them to a kart my brothers had made – using an old car seat and bike wheels nailed to a wooden frame.

It was big enough for me and Elif to sit side-by-side. I had the reins attached to Xabur as pack leader and we would racket around the garden and lanes – laughing and loving our lives.

Hira always wanted to come too, shouting and stretching her chubby little arms out for a lift – but after Elif fell out on a tight bend and scuffed all the skin off her nose and knocked one of her teeth out – my mum said it was too dangerous for the baby.

Because we weren't supposed to be keeping the puppies, my dad had said we shouldn't name them, but me and my sisters knew them like family. There was Fluff, who was the biggest and fattest and softest because he had the longest coat. Although he was the biggest he was also the most gentle so it fell to his smaller but sharper brother to lead the gangly gang of puppies. We nicknamed him Jet because he ran so fast, stretching so low to the ground that you half-expected him to take off like a plane as he disappeared into the distance. Then there were the three little sisters. I say little because, although all the girls were taller than my sisters, they were still a head shorter than their brothers. We called them Cherry, Blossom and Kiwi after the trees in the garden where we played.

CHERRY BLOSSOM FLUFF KIWI JET XENA XABUR

The three girls always stuck together working as a pack within a pack. Realising early on that together they could bring down one of their brothers in a playfight, pinning him to the floor, and nipping and chewing him in victorious delight before racing back to us for safety.

We each had our favourites. For Hira it was loyal mum Princess Xena (named by my brother Azad after a cartoon he loved). Xena often spurned our chariot racing game, preferring, instead, to stay home with Hira. Xena's maternal instinct meant my mum could happily leave her to entertain Hira as she went about tending the garden.

Hira took her first few steps clutching Xena's collar and soon the two of them became a familiar site wobbling round the garden with Hira's little fat fist grasping her fur. If they wandered too far from the house, bossy little Hira would order the obliging Xena to the floor and think nothing of clambering on her back for a ride home – just as our own mother had many years earlier.

For Elif it was Fluff. The gentle giant. Fluff with his big brown eyes and my curly-haired sister with hers, were a match made in heaven. Both were carefree and as cute as could be.

They were inseparable and Elif gave up all other pastimes to play with Fluff. Aside from the chariot racing, they enjoyed swimming and hiking. Elif also liked to dress Fluff in outfits she'd put together, including hats and scarves complemented by plaiting his hair and loading it with clips and bobbles – and once, colouring him in with my mum's lipstick.

My mum was furious when Elif, brandishing a lipstick stub, proudly displayed her handiwork.

"Ta-Dah!" she announced with a flourish and a bow, presenting the lumbering Fluff with a bright red sticky face and clumps of my mum's only lipstick that she'd bought for her sister's wedding, stuck to his nose.

Declaring that red suited him most, Elif set about the very painful and often bloody process of embroidering his name on a kerchief for his neck.

It was painstaking work, which in her typically determined way, she insisted on completing herself. And although, to a critical eye, the end product was a bit wobbly and blood-stained, both she and Fluff were delighted. And from that day on he could be seen from way across the plain – head held high, the red triangle embellished with his name hanging at a jaunty angle from his neck.

Although I loved them all – my favourite was Xabur. I was five when he was born and we had enjoyed a friendship very like Elif and Fluff's.

But over the years ours had grown even stronger. If I was struggling with schoolwork or fretting over a problem I would often find Xabur's warm nose plonked in my lap. He'd fix me with a stare and sigh in sympathy – I was sure – for whatever ailed me. He was a constant companion and my best friend.

He was loyal, strong and clever and after my dad, he loved me most. With my dad away, Xabur had become my shadow – rarely more than two paces from my side – unless he was called away to instil some discipline into his unruly brood who continued to pester the life out of his long-suffering wife.

It never ceased to amaze me that when Xena's nagging growl, my mum's scolding and my sister's angry threats had all failed to still the squabbling puppies – Xabur only had to stand and raise his hackles.

My dad reckoned he made a growl so low that only the other dogs could hear it. Whether he did or not – I will never know – but I knew that just by bristling as he stood, the rest of his obedient pack immediately snapped to attention – as silent and attentive as soldiers on parade.

Rarely did he have to do more – I say rarely because one time does stick in my head. That day, Jet was antagonising Fluff – who was being a good sport as his brother chased around him nipping at his heels and barking in his face.

Fluff entered, good naturedly, into a game of chase, with no hope of outrunning his super-fast sibling.

But by threading his way round the trees, leading Jet on a dance, he managed to shake him off sufficiently to make a break for home and the prospect of a peaceful nap on the verandah.

Quickening his pace, Fluff had reached the orchard before Jet caught up with him and right at that moment Hira wobbled out into their path.

Fluff skidded to a halt at her feet – but Jet, always the more boisterous, leapt straight over her head and spun barking into his brother's face, knocking Hira to the ground as he turned. Oblivious to her squeals, Jet, crowed in triumph over his cowed brother.

Watching from my side on the verandah, Xabur leapt to his feet and flew across the orchard in one almighty bound.

Stunned by his father's presence Jet bowed his head and whimpered some kind of an apology.

But this time a warning was not going to be enough.

As my mother scooped the now sobbing Hira into her arms Xabur turned and stood for a moment over the whimpering Jet.

Endangering people was forbidden – it was a rule my father had taught Xabur as a puppy and now it was clearly time for Jet to learn.

As the other puppies watched on, maybe silently ordered to by their furious father, maybe just entranced by the drama, Xabur threw back his huge head and howled. Like nails down a blackboard, the sound set my teeth on edge.

Then, dropping his head, he fixed Jet with a narrow gaze, curled back his lips to reveal his massive fangs and uttering a low, rumbling growl, that I felt more than heard, he leapt at Jet, knocking him sideways across the dirt, squealing louder than Hira.

Not satisfied yet, Xabur was upon him, rolling him in the dirt, until he had him helpless, on his back – Xabur's fangs round his throat.

For a moment they were locked in this mortal combat – terrified Jet, whimpering, Xabur dominant, teeth squeezing and pinching the soft flesh of Jet's throat as he continued to rumble a low warning.

Remembering cuffs I'd had round the ear from my dad in the past – I knew that the blow itself didn't really hurt – the humiliation was the most painful.

And sure enough Xabur prolonged the punishment until terrified Jet peed on the spot.

Recognising victory and absolute obedience, Xabur waited a moment longer before turning on his heel and walking back to my side with a slightly apologetic shrug and an expression that I took to mean 'that'll teach him'.

Battered and bruised, Jet slunk after his father, lying flat on the floor at a respectful distance, watching for any sign of forgiveness.

And that's where he stayed for the rest of the afternoon – shunned by the rest of the pack, who knew better than to get on the wrong side of the mighty Xabur.

It's easy for me to write about the dogs – but sharing with you about how we left them is a little harder.

Faced with such a miserable task it was Grandpa Cevit who came up with a plan.

Unable to take any of the livestock with us, Grandpa Cevit and two other old men from our village militia agreed to use our dogs to herd all the sheep right up to the higher plains. At least up there the sheep and cattle could continue to graze, the dogs could hunt and roam free and when we returned we could round them all up again – well that was the plan.

Elif didn't like it one bit.

My biro was running out. I shook it, then sucked the nib, but there was no ink left – so I fished in my bag for a pencil Sydrah had found and given to me.

Writing about leaving the dogs was hard – bringing the memories of the misery flooding back. Closing my eyes I recalled Elif's fury at the prospect.

"How will he know when to come back? How will he know where we are?" she demanded. Hira wailed and clung to Xena.

Xabur was equally unsure – eyeing Grandpa Cevit suspiciously and looking to me for reassurance.

Holding his great big head in my hands and scratching behind his ears I tried to find a way to tell him we weren't abandoning him.

"I promise we'll be back. I promise," I repeated as tears started to roll down my cheeks. "You have to be smart Xabur," I urged him. "Stay away from the people. Stay safe. We'll be back," I repeated as my voice started to wobble.

At one point I thought he understood, and then I thought he looked sad, then reproachful and then it was all too much and I collapsed sobbing, arms round his neck, breathing the comfortable warm scent of dog as I buried my face in his fur.

Blinking away tears I picked up the pencil and carried on writing.

What a sight we must have been – me and my sisters sobbing, unashamedly, for the loss of our furry family.

Grandpa Cevit took them up to the furthest field so they wouldn't see us leave and follow us. We had walked at least a mile and completely out of sight when we heard their howling across the plains. They called and strained for us – their cries carried on the wind to us as we joined the sad procession of our friends and family to safety.

Looking back as we left, seeing all the misery around us, I could taste my hatred for the ratmen.

14. THE DEMENTORS

We walked in miserable silence for a while before a little voice piped up, "Dogs not happy then Dilly?"

Trotting to keep up was my cousin Diyar*. I smiled down at him and just shook my head.

At eight, with goggly glasses and spiky hair, Diyar was the double of his idol, the boy wizard, Harry Potter.

Harry Potter was on his T-shirt and his backpack – he'd read every one of the books and had even tried to arrange a Quidditch match last summer.

Although his passion for the boy wizard made him a bit of an oddity in our village – Diyar remained undaunted.

"This reminds me of the return of Voldemort and the rise of the Death Eaters," he said, shaking his head.

"No one wanted to believe what was happening then either," he frowned at me. "Did they Dilly?"

He looked up at me for reassurance and I winced, knowing his Pottermania was my fault. How could I forget? It was only a few years ago that I had gained legendary

* PRONUNCIATION *D-R*

status in the village thanks to the boy wizard, myself.

At the age of ten, much to the delight of my whole family, I had won the maths prize in our village.

To be honest I didn't really find it that difficult. Like I said before, not all the children could go to school and most who did were the boys. By the age of ten I was one of the few remaining girls in the school and it wasn't particularly hard to be top. It was either me or my cousin, Beritan – we took it in turns and the boys were fine about it.

$5 \times 5 = 25$

$6 \times 6 = 36$

$12 \times 7 = 84.$

They spent their free time playing football or fighting and as there were only three of us girls and we didn't like either football or fighting we used to sit on a bench in the yard and play schools, taking it in turn to be the teacher and orchestrating times tables chanting and spellings.

It had started as a game from when we were little but over the years we had got faster and faster and better and better.

Like my dad said, "Practice makes perfect." And without really realising – it did.

Coming top in the maths test meant that I was sent to represent Rojava at the Lanaco Kanton test. This was to involve children from hundreds of schools in the area and although I was pleased at all the attention and praise I was getting, I didn't really expect to get very far in the competition.

You can imagine my surprise, when my times tables speed took me through the first four rounds – knocking out hundreds of others on the way.

The final came down to me and an older boy from a village to the south of Lanaco.

He was very good – older than me with a round face and chubby.

Good he might have been – but quick he wasn't. Before the final, Beritan, who'd been weighing up the opposition, sidled up to me and said, "Close your eyes and imagine it's me... you'll thrash him!" And I did.

By winning the regional heats I'd qualified for the Syrian National Maths Test in Damascus itself.

Part of the regional prize included a round trip bus ticket for me and my dad to our capital city.

I had never been and was very excited at seeing life outside our village and Lanaco for the first time ever.

We travelled overnight on the bus – arriving in Damascus at 5.30am.

Dad took me for lentil soup for breakfast and once we'd eaten and found the venue for the competition we still had hours left before the start.

That's when my brilliant dad hit upon the idea of going to the cinema. We'd seen billboards announcing the first Syrian translation of the Harry Potter film – and I'm not sure which of us was more excited at the prospect of seeing it.

We walked the half hour to the cinema, hand-in-hand and happy. After buying the tickets, my dad handed me a box of popcorn.

"This'll be your prize, Dilly," he beamed at me.

"I haven't won yet Dad," I laughed.

"Shhh," he held his finger to his lips. "Don't spoil our first film with irrelevant facts."

And it was only then that I realised it was my dad's first time at the cinema too.

We didn't talk much after that, just sat in awestruck silence, mindlessly eating the popcorn as we were transported into the magical world of wizardry and witchcraft.

We left the cinema, still holding hands in silence, took part in the maths tournament, which had paled into insignificance by then, (I did well – coming in the top twenty and winning a prize of books for our school), and it wasn't 'til we were on the bus home that we started to speak. Slowly at first remembering little details that had delighted us, the people waving and smiling in photos, the sorting hat, the sweets, broomstick riding – there was so much. We talked for almost the whole journey – my dad just as delighted and as excited as me at the incredible, breathtaking magical world that we felt like we'd both visited.

At the end my dad said, "I wish I could have gone to that school."

"Me too," I agreed.

"I feel a bit sad now that it's finished," he added. "Like I miss it already!"

"But it's not finished, Dad!" I exclaimed. "That's just the film of the first book. There's lots more still to come."

The look of delight on my dad's face made me feel like the tables had turned and I was the parent.

"There's more than one? That's incredible," he shook his head in disbelief, before adding, "Well Dilly, you'd best keep practising your maths so we have an excuse to get back and watch the next one!"

And it was my trip to the cinema that gained me legendary status in the village that summer.

I was the only child to have been to the cinema and tried to recreate the whole film for my friends – so they could share the joy.

I must have retold the Harry Potter story over one thousand times – with many of the little kids wanting to hear their favourite parts over and over again.

Diyar was completely overawed by the whole story and would trail round the village after me, asking question after question about spells and wands, to which I mostly had to make up the answers.

Harry Potter fervour gripped the village that summer with most of us fashioning our own wands out of sticks and creating our own brand of magic and mayhem.

Like most things, the fad passed. But not for Diyar, who pestered his parents until they bought him the whole series of books. With hindsight I'm not sure it was a good idea because three years on and Diyar is, if anything, even more obsessed with the boy wizard.

Me and my dad never went to see another film. Things started to change for the worse in Syria after that. We did, though, read the books bought for Diyar and followed Harry's quest to its triumphant end.

And so it was that Diyar and I walked side by side, in the sad little procession of our families as we fled the sickening spread of the caliphate.

"It's just like it, isn't it Dilly?" Diyar continued, unaware that I'd been lost in thought for the last few minutes and not really listening to what he'd been saying. "That's why I've brought my wand," he illustrated with a flourish of the knobbly stick he was carrying.

"Yes, you can never be too careful," I agreed.

"I mean the ratmen – they're just the same as the Dementors," Diyar continued, now quoting lengthy extracts from the books from memory.

"Dementors are among the foulest creatures that walk this earth. They infest the darkest, filthiest places, they glory in decay and despair,

they drain peace, hope and happiness out of the air around them...
Get too near a Dementor and every good feeling, every happy memory
will be sucked out of you. If it can, the Dementor will feed on you
long enough to reduce you to something like itself... soulless and evil.
You will be left with nothing but the worst experiences of your life."

And by now Diyar did have my full attention. It was so true –
an exact description of the miserable, hateful plague of ratmen that
were swarming across Syria. How hadn't I seen it before? They even
looked like Dementors with their black uniform, grey skin and angry
faces. We were being attacked by Dementors – and without magic
to fight back.

"I've been practising my Patronus Charm," Diyar said with another
flourish of his stick. "It's the only thing that will stop them you know."

I smiled down at him nodding – wishing there was a spell that
could magic away the advancing Dementors from our village.

"How have you practised?" I asked –
half-hoping that he did have some magical
powers.

"You have to fight back with happiness
and love," Diyar asserted. "You have to think
of your happiest memory until the joy oozes
out of you – they can't bear that."

"What's your happiest memory, Diyar?"

"That's easy," he grinned. "When your
brothers showed me the secret water chute
– that was, without doubt, the happiest
day of my life."

The secret water chute was part of a
network of caves that littered the cliffside
behind our house. People used to live in the caves and we still used
them to store food and keep it cool through the summer.

There was a small track that led down from the back of our house descending the overgrown cliff face and here you could find over two dozen cave openings.

We'd played in some of the bigger ones for years – some were forbidden to us as they were too dangerous. That obviously hadn't stopped my brothers from investigating them over the years and what they discovered turned out to be our own magical secret that we kept from the adults.

Inside some of the forbidden caves were deep dark holes that seemed to have no bottom. If you dropped stones in them you could hear them ricocheting off the edges and in to the centre of the universe – we were sure.

My brothers and their friends had spent years investigating the labyrinth of caves until they made their best discovery.

By dropping coloured balls down the bottomless hole they eventually discovered that it came out into a hidden pool feeding the river below us.

Further investigation revealed the constant trickle of mountain water washing through it had smoothed the inside of the hole all the way down.

It was my brother Azad first, with a rope tied round his waist, who made the descent into the black hole and quickly disappeared round the bend.

As Nuri and Sela were letting out more rope, me and Bilal raced down to the river and within seconds, whooping with delight, Azad appeared out of an unseen hole and plopped into the river.

"It's brilliant!" he screamed. "It's completely black inside but smooth and slippy and it twists and turns," he said, racing to the side to have another go.

We were cautious at first, but within the hour, we'd abandoned the rope and all of us had leapt into the hole and slipped and slid and screamed all the way down to the water.

Climbing out, wet and waterlogged, was the hardest thing. It took team work and much slipping and scrabbling to make it back up to the path – but it was worth it.

We knew the adults would forbid us from sliding. Girls and boys weren't even supposed to swim in the same part of the river. So we only told our cousins who could swim and we were all sworn to protect the secret chute.

From then on, when the heat and dust of the village got too much, we would tell our parents that we were going to sit in the cool of the caves.

It wasn't a complete lie. We did go to the caves – but there was no sitting. One by one we'd leap into the chute and squeal with delight as we spun through the darkness before plunging into the ice cold water below. It was brilliant fun.

Diyar had only been allowed to join in for the last couple of summers since he could swim – but it was the one thing that could prize his head out of a Harry Potter book – the secret chute was that good. I'm not surprised he'd picked it as his happiest memory.

As we trudged on towards Lanaco and the relative safety of my aunties' house, (the ones who sold food to travellers), I found myself wondering about the arrival of the ratmen.

I feared that Diyar's happy memories and stick wand wouldn't be enough to protect him from these very real Dementors who were sucking the joy out of our world. But somewhere deep down inside I knew that, even without the use of magic, it would be the love that united us that would ultimately defeat them.

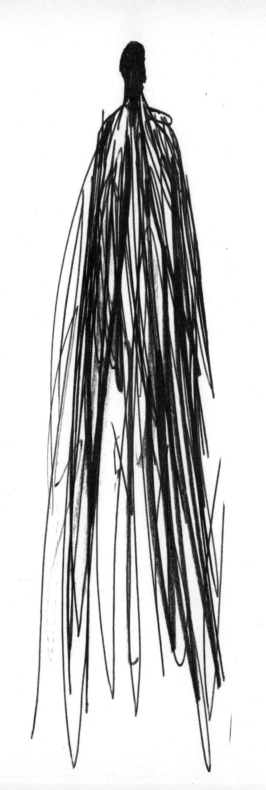

15. Leaving the Courtyard

I stopped writing and used one of the valuable pages of my book to draw a picture of a Dementor ratman – it was such a vivid image – part myth, part real-life monster. I scribbled over and over to darken the drawing and realised my wrist was aching from all the writing and I was getting a lumpy sore bit on my finger from pressing down on the pencil.

Stashing my book and pencil in my bag, I hooked it over my shoulder as I stood up.

I plucked a couple of pomegranates from the tree and put them in my bag as well, before going in search of Rehana.

Ercan told me she'd gone up to the top corner to practise with her new super-duper rifle. Peering out of the door in the courtyard wall I spotted Abdullah helping unload supplies of crates from a truck.

Catching my eye he called to me and said, "Tell Rehana when this is unloaded they'll give you a lift to the crossing. Be about half an hour."

I nodded and headed up the hill to the top corner where I could see Rehana and the YPJ girls.

Rehana was lying in the dust, propped up on her elbows with her rifle in front of her.

She was firing through a hole in the wall at enemy positions below. Next to her the other girls were using a free-standing mortar to attack the same position where the snipers were hiding.

Watching them work fascinated me. They were all so

confident and capable they could even talk and joke as they took the fight to our enemy. Among the many things the ratmen hate are women. They believe that if they're killed by a woman they will go straight to hell and so, of course, we do our very best to oblige.

I watched Songul snip through the binding on the shells and hand them to Sydrah who popped them, one at a time, into the top of the mortar.

"Can I fire, Commander?" she asked each time of Rehana, who gave the order while continuing to fire her own rifle.

A group of girls happy in their work – they could just as easily have been sitting in the garden, shelling peas with my mum.

Seeing me approach they told Rehana, who shuffled back from her position to a safe spot behind the building. She was flushed but grinning from ear to ear.

"You gotta try this, Dilly," she sighed in awe as she stroked her laser-guided rifle. "It's like nothing you've ever fired before. It's incredible."

The rifle was long and propped up on a small tripod attached to the barrel which was projecting through a hole in the wall. Rolling to the far side, Rehana gestured for me to take up her firing position with my shoulder to the butt of the rifle.

Lying in the dirt, the feel of the gun against my shoulder was familiar to me. I'd been shooting since I could walk, more or less. I ran my hand down the stock until I reached the trigger and squinting my left eye I peered through the sights.

Lying next to me Rehana explained the differences between

this and the Russian issue AK47s and Kalashnikovs that we were used to.

It was more powerful but the real difference was in the sights. By squeezing the trigger as you focused, a little red dot would appear on your target. It was like the laser pens that the boys annoyed us with at school.

I'd picked a spot on the outside of the house they were targeting and watched through the crosshairs on the sights as the little red dot danced on the wall.

"Aim for that satellite dish on the roof," said Rehana. "They're using it for communication. See if you can blast it to bits."

I moved the sights a fraction and the little dot jumped onto the satellite dish.

"Try and keep it still and when you're sure you're ready then squeeze the trigger all the way back to fire," said Rehana.

Focusing, concentrating, remembering everything my dad and brothers had taught me about shooting, I took a breath, held it and squeezed the trigger right back. I wasn't sure what to expect – I knew Rehana was raving about it – so you can imagine my surprise when absolutely nothing happened.

I heard Rehana whisper, "Patience…" then 'BOOM' the satellite dish exploded in front of my eyes.

"Isn't it brilliant?" she marvelled. "It decides when to fire. You pick the target and when you squeeze the trigger it sends and receives messages from the target to the gun over fifty times in a second."

"What messages?" I asked.

"Oh it checks wind speed and weather conditions – it even allows for the curvature of the earth.

"You pick the target but it picks the shot. You could shoot the eyebrows off a gnat at fifty paces with this thing. It's brilliant. Ain't no stopping me now," she giggled as she collapsed the tripod, slid the barrel from the hole in the wall and rolled back behind the building.

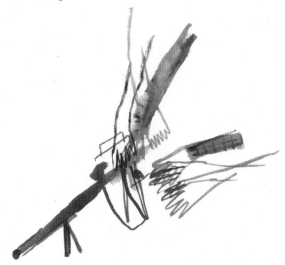

Following her off the ridge I gave her Abdullah's message and said we only had about ten minutes left.

Using the rifle sling Rehana swung it onto her back and shouldered the rounds of ammo she'd been given.

Hugging the girls she promised not to forget all the supplies they'd asked for from Turkey. Before we left I hugged them all too wishing I could stay with them and fight.

"Right, Sydrah's in charge while I'm away," said Rehana. "Be brave but do not be stupid and do not get yourselves killed or you'll have me to answer to! That's an order," she commanded.

"Right Sir, yessir," chorused the girls. "Go and enjoy your holiday Rehana – we'll hold the fort."

As we turned to go Sydrah cupped her hand to her mouth and broke into the ululating war cry of the YPJ that struck fear in our enemy – but made us smile as we walked back down the hill to the courtyard.

I didn't have anything to pack, so I helped Rehana collect the things she thought we might need and pack them in her rucksack.

The injured boys had already been put on the truck to be taken to a secret clinic that would treat them in Turkey and so the courtyard was empty now and before I left I took a moment to drink in the beauty of the pomegranate tree, laden with its ruby jewels and its promise of hope for a better future.

16. THE GATE TO NOWHERE

Bundled into the back of the truck with Rehana and some of the injured we waited for clearance from the patrols that the road ahead was safe to pass and I used the time to update my diary.

I felt bewildered by how fast things changed.

Rehana reassured me that Lanaco was clear, for the time being at least. Problem was their big guns were ranged on the hill behind us and were targeting moving vehicles. We timed our trip to coincide with another airstrike on those positions which sent them running for cover and within minutes we were on the lower road out of Lanaco – heading back towards my aunties' house and the turning for Rojava.

I wanted to go home. I wanted to go home so much I thought I would burst as we reached the turning, or just burst into tears. How could we be so close to my home and yet so far away at the same time, with all the people that made it home scatterered to the four winds?

It was a silent trip.

I was miserable and feeling sorry for myself again. But, for once, no one seemed to notice or try to cheer me up, which was a relief. And it's a wonder how fast those feelings can change.

We couldn't cross the border at the normal checkpoint because the Turks had closed it. They didn't like us and certainly didn't want to help us. People reckon the Turks hoped that we'd be wiped out by the ratmen and save them the bother.

I'd known about the border crossing – I even knew people were waiting at the gate, hoping the Turks might relent and let them cross to safety. But I hadn't imagined the sight that greeted us as we swept round the last bend on the road to Turkey.

There were thousands of people. More people than I'd ever seen gathered together in one place before.

It was a field of people. A carpet of Kurds. It looked as if they had been planted in the no man's land between Lanaco and Turkey.

Like stalks of wheat waiting to be plucked to safety, they just stood and waited. And they'd been waiting for days. Twenty-five apparently. Well I stopped feeling sorry for myself just at the sight of them. I was still full from my breakfast of cheese and watermelon and bread. I'd slept on a mattress – warm and safe – that, alone, made me far better off than these people.

Rehana had some messages to deliver and things to do – so I waited in the truck for a while – watching the wheat people.

I knew we would cross the border in secret under the cover of darkness and wondered why all these people didn't do the same.

But there were so many of them – I don't suppose you could sneak 20,000 people under a fence without them being noticed.

As the sun started to sink behind the mountains to the west, it took the heat with it and the prickling cold started to settle in for the night.

In the field people started to stamp their feet and draw closer together. They reminded me of a documentary I'd seen once about penguins in Antarctica who huddle together for warmth in a big group through the winter, each taking a turn on the cold outside edge of the group before slowly inching to the middle to warm up. I wondered how they survived.

When Rehana returned, all her errands completed, we drove along the fence-line, heading back towards Rojava.

Here the fence was littered with oil tankers, tractors, even combine-harvesters. Their owners, too terrified to leave them to be destroyed, had driven them to the border but could go no further and many were now living in them.

We waited for nightfall at the nearest spot to where we would later cross the border. Parked near tractor-town I watched the families who were living in their machinery.

A pregnant woman, who had at least six children, waved

and smiled to us – beckoning us to join her at her tractor.

We had nothing else to do, so taking one of the precious pomegranates from my bag, Rehana and I wandered over for a chat.

Her name was Zelal and both she and her children were delighted to see us. She apologised for not offering us tea – but water was in short supply in the field and was being rationed. They hadn't had a drink all day.

Zelal offered the tractor step as a seat to Rehana (her YPJ status made her a very honoured visitor) and spread a blanket on the ground for the rest of us.

Rehana shared round her water canteen and I was surprised that the little kids didn't just gulp it all down – not having drunk all day. Clearly they'd been here long enough to know better than to squander rations.

Producing the pomegranate brought squeals of delight from the children. I handed it to Zelal but she declined, patting her stomach – suggesting she was already full – and nodded for me to share it with the children as she chatted to Rehana.

Breaking it open I offered the fruit round to the collection of youngsters who gently eased out a few seeds each and popped them in their mouths.

Nobody spoke but as the richness of the seeds burst in their mouths they grinned at each other in delight.

One of the smallest children wobbled over to me and plonked herself on my lap with a smile, opening her mouth like a baby bird for me to drop in more pomegranate pearls.

Their interest in me lasted as long as the fruit did and when the husk had been sucked dry one by one they drifted back to playing in the mud – except for the baby. Clearly satisfied by her meagre meal she'd dropped off to sleep on my lap.

Not long afterwards, Rehana said it was time to go and

Zelal picked the sleeping girl from my lap and popped her into the tractor cab wrapped in our picnic blanket for warmth.

"Well, that's one down," she beamed happily at me.

"How long have you been here?" I asked.

"Today is our 25th day."

"How do you manage to keep warm at night? It's so cold – how are you going to manage with the baby?"

"We snuggle together for warmth, wrapped up in whatever we have. Fortunately there's plenty of us," she grinned, reminding me again of the penguins.

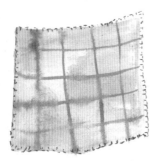

"The baby will be fine – I'll hold him in my arms and keep him warm like that." She was so cheerful, I just nodded and smiled.

"When's it due?" asked Rehana.

"Last week," laughed Zelal. "Not in a rush to get here, obviously," she added, laughing again at her little joke.

"But I'm all prepared," she continued, reaching behind the tractor wheel and producing her baby bag.

With great pride and reverence she showed us the hand-knitted, baby shawl, clean and white and pristine. She laid out the baby's outfit on her lap, smoothing it with her fingers and swatting the other children away – forbidding them to touch it with their muddy hands.

I glanced up at Rehana to see if she found the whole thing as desperately sad as me, but if she did, she didn't show it. Marvelling at the stitching on the blanket and helping to pack things away before hugging Zelal and wishing her luck as if it were another normal day in the village. For her part, Zelal was delighted. I don't think I'd ever met a more cheerful woman in my life.

As we headed back to the truck I realised her cheerfulness had put me to shame.

The Dementors certainly hadn't sucked the joy out of her life, and her easy, happy nature had definitely set a good example to her contented kids. I vowed to try and be less grumpy and told Rehana, which made her laugh out loud, so that was a good start.

We still had more waiting to do and I took the chance to write about my meeting with Zelal and her family living in their tractor.

I felt sure that this was what Rehana had meant when she first told me to "write it all down." She was right – people should know about Zelal and her children. Maybe our nasty neighbours didn't care but maybe there were some nice people out there in the world who would help.

I struggled to explain the awfulness of their situation, but thought it was important to put in all the facts I'd gleaned.

She'd been there for twenty-five days. I checked the clock on the truck dashboard and realised I'd been writing for seventeen minutes.

Time for a quick sum. So there's sixty minutes in an hour. 24 hours in a day – that's 24 x 60 = 1,440. So 25 days would be 25 x 1,440 = 36,000 minutes.

She'd been sat here, in this field for 36,000 minutes and she was still smiling. I looked back at the pages I'd written in the last seventeen minutes. Several pages of my precious book and enough to make the corn on my finger throb, I worked out that I would have time to write them another 2,117 times to match the amount of time Zelal had spent right here in this field. It made my mind boggle at the prospect. And Zelal was still smiling. I made a note to myself from Zelal on the inside

cover of my diary in big bubble writing and coloured it in.
I determined to make it my new motto.

HAVE HOPE
AND BE
HAPPY

17. MINES, TUNNELS & TURKEY

Night falls suddenly in Syria. One minute I was happily writing away – the next it was pitch black and time to go.

I was aware of a flurry of messages between Rehana and YPG controls in Lanaco and over the border in Turkey. We were told to wait at a certain safe-point.

The truck driver took us to the spot and had clearly been there before – but it's very difficult to drive in the dark without lights on, so we kind of crept there very slowly.

As my eyes became more accustomed to the dark I began to try and scan my surroundings and see if I could work out where we were. It wasn't far from the turning to Rojava. Then, as the moon peeped briefly from behind a cloud it lit up the river and suddenly I recognised our exact location. We were at the top of the track where we'd seen my dad and brothers stop and sing back to us across the valley. Squinting out to the river I tried to make out the shape of our house on the hillside but the moon retreated behind the clouds and it was too dark.

Suddenly Rehana got the go-ahead. She'd already changed out of her YPJ jacket, swapping it for a big baggy jumper with a roll neck that she'd produced from her rucksack. As she pulled it over her head and scooped her hair out of the back I watched the soldier disappear, replaced by the village girl I'd known my whole life.

She refused, point blank, to be separated from her new super-duper rifle, so we had to cut a hole in the side of her rucksack so the end of the barrel could poke out. By sliding it through the sleeve of her jacket and knotting the end of the sleeve it was camouflaged.

The driver, Jan, led us up the track a few yards before stopping.

"OK – this is where we leave the track and start to cross the minefield…"

"Mines?" Horrified, I turned to Rehana.

Seeing the look of terror on my face she explained, "Yeah I didn't tell you about the mines – I didn't want to frighten you."

"It's fine," Jan interrupted. "I cross here almost every day. I know a safe path. You just have to follow me. Stay in line and try and put your feet where I do. I'll go first, then you Dilvan, then Rehana – OK?"

Clearly the look on my face showed that I wasn't OK, so he added, "Look – we've worked hard to clear this route and we're fairly certain we've removed all the mines – we just don't take any chances. We know there's loads more mines further away in the field and they can move about under the ground in the water table. So stick to the route."

Clearly bored and cold, Rehana poked me in the back hissing, "If you don't get a move on we'll freeze to death anyway… move."

That was an order.

With my hand on Jan's shoulder and Rehana's on mine we inched across the open field towards a rise covered in trees.

"Left…" hissed Rehana.

"Left what?"

"Left foot you idiot. We need to march in line together. As Jan lifts his left foot, put yours where it was – OK? That way we reduce the risk of stepping on a mine."

It only took a couple of minutes to reach the rise. Jan took small steps and after a while I kind of got the hang of it but

I was very glad to get out of the minefield.

Following Jan up the rise he stopped where a tree was growing out of the rocks and scrabbling around the roots he suddenly revealed a cave opening – just like the ones behind our house.

The opening wasn't big – not even a metre wide. Jan squeezed through and dropped out of sight then hissed at me to follow him.

Lying on my stomach, I lowered my legs through the hole and felt Jan's arms below, guiding me. Wriggling backwards 'til I was just gripping the opening with my fingers I dropped into the hole.

Rehana dropped her rucksack down to Jan then jumped down to join us. Once inside, Jan produced a torch and I saw we were in a cavern – tall enough to stand in. Tree roots and branches cluttered the opening and ahead of us two narrow passages led off in different directions.

Jan smiled at us and nodded. Talking was forbidden. This passage was a lifeline for the people of Lanaco. Jan had told me earlier that they used it to get the sick and injured out to safety and also to get emergency supplies in. I was well aware that noise echoes in caves and we weren't far from the Turkish border – which was swarming with their soldiers and we didn't want to alert them to our secret route round their locked border gate.

Following Jan down the passage on the left, his torch lit up the tunnel ahead.

The ground was uneven but not too bad. There were places where the cave narrowed and Jan had to stoop to pass – some bits were even a struggle for Rehana to squeeze through with her rucksack but on the whole I could walk upright for pretty much most of the way.

I realised, after we'd been going for about twenty minutes that I could see light ahead of us and the tunnel widened. Here it was big enough to drive a truck through and hanging on the walls, gas lamps placed at regular intervals made it much easier to see where you were walking.

Crates and equipment were stacked here and it was clear the tunnel was in regular use. Not much further down and Jan turned off from the main tunnel into a narrow passage but it was well lit and at the end was a flight of steps leading up to a trap door.

Feeling along the wall, Jan grabbed a tree root, which turned out to be attached to a rope. Three good pulls on the rope and seconds later the trapdoor sprang open and light streamed down the steps into the tunnel.

"Azadiya Kurdistan," said a voice.

"Azadiya Kurdistan," we replied as we made our way up the stairs and into Turkey.

18. Semikan, stew and pyjamas

We'd arrived in the kitchen of a small house that was full to bursting with Kurdish men. There must have been at least sixty men in the house – talking, smoking, making plans. Jan greeted a few of them by name but seemed in a hurry to move on and we followed him straight out of the house, where even more men were huddled in groups. The little house was the only building in the area and I realised it must belong to a farmer who worked the fields on the Turkish side of the border.

Once outside Jan quickly spied the friend he was looking for standing by a white car parked in the field behind the house.

No one seemed bothered by our arrival or by our leaving – and as we drove away across the bumpy field I thought the little house was rather like a tiny bus station – where strangers met and milled around, waiting for the next leg of their journey.

The car driver was called Yahya. He was a Turkish Kurd who lived in the nearby town of Semikan* and he was also Jan's cousin.

As we drove the five minute journey from the border into Semikan, Yahya explained that General Zinar had asked him, personally, to look after me and Rehana as his guests. He was clearly flattered to have been asked such a favour by the general and determined to do his best to make us as comfortable as possible.

It was the early hours of the morning when we pulled up

* PRONUNCIATION *Shemi-kaan*

104

outside his apartment building and were bundled indoors.

As we climbed the stairs, Yahya explained that there were three apartments in the building.

They'd given over his mother's apartment on the ground floor to two families of refugees from Lanaco. His mother now stayed with his brother Mehmet and his family on the first floor, while Yahya and his family, including us, were on the top floor.

Hearing us on the stairs his wife flung the door open and came out to greet us and with her came the smell of cooking.

We placed our shoes by the door and she ushered us inside to a sitting room with a couple of squashy sofas, an electric fire and a big flat screen TV on the wall. Her name was Ipek and she was very friendly.

Within minutes we were sitting drinking tea with Yahya and Jan while Ipek, who was pregnant, brought in food and laid it out on a cloth on the floor.

There were individual bowls of steaming lamb stew and a large decorated platter with bulgar rice topped with fried chicken, a dish of chopped salad and fresh bread, of course.

Rehana, Jan and Yahya chatted as I watched Ipek place spoons for each of us on the cloth and pour frothy yoghurt into glasses to drink.

I was so hungry and the sight and smell of food made my mouth water. I snapped it shut so I didn't dribble but my stomach rumbled and growled so loudly it drowned out Rehana's conversation.

"Sorry," I apologised as everyone turned to look at me in surprise.

But they burst out laughing and Ipek was immediately dragging me to the floor and urging me to eat.

"The poor child's starving," she

exclaimed, sitting me down next to her and handing me a spoon.

I didn't need telling twice, although I did say a quick prayer for the tractor children I'd left starving in that field only a couple of hours ago.

It had been a long time since I'd eaten anything that good and the four of us ate in silence – enjoying every bit of Ipek's feast.

The lamb stew was slow cooked with carrots and potatoes – just like my mum's. I spooned some over the rice and loved the familiar taste. Eating crispy chicken with our fingers and helping ourselves to salad – all you could hear was crunching and chewing. It's amazing the difference food makes.

By the time we'd finished there wasn't a scrap left – even the gravy had been wiped from the bowls with the bread.

The Ayran, the yoghurt drink, was frothy and very slightly salty. I gulped it down and wiped away the moustache of yoghurt bubbles on my sleeve. Catching my arm, Ipek surveyed the state of the checked shirt I wore over my T-shirt. It was stiff with a crust of dirt.

Sniffing her disapproval she lumbered to her feet and disappeared. Together we stacked the empty bowls in the kitchen and folded up the cloth as Ipek arrived back with two sets of fluffy cotton pyjamas.

Handing them to me and Rehana she said, "You both look exhausted. Sleep now and I'll wash your clothes and have them ready for you when you wake up. You can shower in the morning and start the day afresh."

Jan was leaving – heading back to Lanaco, Yahya was driving him back to the tunnel house and Rehana walked down to the car to talk about secret stuff.

A 24-hour Turkish news channel was flickering on the TV. For the first time in a long time I was warm, comfortable and full and suddenly I felt exhausted.

Taking the pyjamas from Ipek, I hugged her tight and thanked her for her kindness. She hugged me back, resting her chin on the top of my head and swaying gently for a minute before saying, "No need for thanks. We're in this together – I just wish I could do more for all the others."

She disappeared again and arrived back with two bedrolls. Together we unrolled them on the floor in front of the little fire and covered each of them with a sheet and pillow. There was a fleecy blanket for both of us and when Ipek was satisfied that everything was ready she kissed me on the head, told me to put my dirty clothes outside the door and headed back to the kitchen to finish clearing up the dinner things before starting the washing.

I sat on the couch and undressed. My trousers were so filthy they could virtually stand up on their own. The pyjamas smelt fresh, a scent of flowers and soap powder. It was delicious. They were so clean and soft that I buried my face in them and inhaled. Ipek had put them in front of the fire and slipping my arms inside them was like a warm cuddle.

I bundled all my things together and put them outside the door before peering out of the window to see if Rehana was coming.

The Turkish TV news said it was 3.05am but it was still dark outside and I couldn't see a thing.

Like the pyjamas, the sheets and pillow smelt clean and fresh and although I'd intended to wait up for Rehana – I was asleep before the TV clock clicked to 3.06am.

19. BATTERIES RECHARGED

I don't remember a sleep like that before or since. It was the deepest, most relaxing and most refreshing. I felt like a smartphone, bright and brilliant again after being recharged.

I did wake up at one point – I was thirsty and needed the loo and the house was quiet. Rehana was sleeping next to me. The sound of the washing machine told me that our clothes weren't ready so after relishing the luxury of a glass of water, ice-cold from the fridge, I slipped back under the still warm fleecy blanket and slept again.

When we woke, it was already afternoon. Hearing us stir, Ipek arrived with tea and a hot pan of fried eggs, sausages and fresh crusty bread. There were cheeses, olives, tomatoes, cucumber, yoghurt – in fact everything you need for the perfect breakfast was spread before us on the cloth.

I was so overwhelmed by her kindness and generosity that I couldn't speak, but before I took a mouthful I flung my arms round Ipek and hugged her again – this time in tears.

She was slightly taken aback by the tears until Rehana said, "Ignore her – she gets emotional about food. She loves it that much she wants to eat EVERY day. It's become a habit!"

"Well you've come to the right house for that," smiled Ipek, stroking my hair. "Now come on – tuck in before it gets cold."

Thrusting a crust of bread into the eggs I scooped up a mouthful of sausage and yolk and as I chewed, the familiar sweet warmth made me smile.

"See, what did I tell you – she's a food addict," declared
Rehana. "She just can't get enough of the stuff!"

We all laughed – but it's true. It's hard to be happy when
you're hungry.

Breakfast was a triumph, soon followed by another – a hot
shower and hair wash with shampoo AND conditioner.

Standing under the stream of water, even I was surprised
to see what dropped out of my hair. There was a dead beetle,
bits of twig, lots of brick dust and grit from the bomb blast
in Lanaco and a button! I've no idea where that came from or
how long it had been there.

But standing under the water I soaped and scrubbed and
rinsed until the water ran clear and I felt clean and tingly all over.

Ipek had piled my clean, dry and ironed clothes on a plastic
chair in the bathroom. Newly washed, the faded khaki jeans
were even tighter and shorter but the white T-shirt was white
again and the checked shirt was soft on my skin and no longer
stiff with dirt.

Ipek had found some thick socks and after towel drying my
hair and combing it through I felt as good as new and certainly
able to keep my vow without really having to try. I was happy.

Rehana had showered before me and was also clearly in high
spirits being clean and refreshed and full. She grinned and
nodded her approval when she saw me.

"Come on, let's go and discover Semikan," she said sticking
out her hand to me.

And after slipping on my old boots, which Ipek had found
new laces for, we ran down the stairs together laughing and
joking like we were back in our village.

Yes, we were both happy and hopeful – well, until that is,
we went out on the streets.

20. THE FUGEES

We were still laughing as we burst out of the apartment door and on to the street – but we stopped short, for the noise of our laughter shattered the silence. The deafening silence of Semikan.

It was like we'd burst onto a stage in front of a disappointed audience.

There were people everywhere. From every crack, every corner and every crevice – little faces, old faces, dirty faces and sad faces – stared at us in silence.

Our laughter had disturbed them. So we stopped. We both just stood for a moment sucking up the street scene, staring back at them.

And when the silence had settled back into place – they went on about their business – mostly sitting, staring, waiting.

It wasn't a bad atmosphere. No one seemed angry. Just a little disturbed by our loud laughter.

We turned left and wandered up the street. Semikan is just a one street town – a main street with shops and stores, barbers and cafés. It's much bigger than Rojava but tiny compared to Lanaco.

One main street, with residential streets unfolding either side. But the streets and the shops and the houses were hard to distinguish under the tide of refugees.

Semikan was a town of 50,000 people and since the attack on Lanaco its streets had been swelled by 180,000 refugees – wherever you looked, wherever you turned – this was Fugee Town.

As we walked on further we passed families. The luckier ones living in empty shops or in garages and others just on the street. Old men and women and thousands of children just perched on a piece of mud or gathered on a forecourt.

Life in Semikan tried to continue as normal, but it struggled to do so under the weight of its new visitors. The local people were still out and about, shopping, working, running errands and taking their kids to school. They were just being watched by the thousands of eyes of the Fugees. People who had no home to clean or food to cook. They just sat and watched – as if their life was on pause. Waiting. Staring into space. Preoccupied by their own thoughts.

A queue outside the barbers blocked the pavement. Bearded men of all ages seemed in a desperate rush for a shave.

The queue parted to let us pass and I wondered if there was a special offer on shaving in Semikan that day – but hearing the men talk I realised they were all desperate to remove their traditional beards – anything that reminded them of our hated enemy – the ratmen.

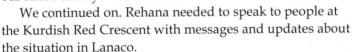

We continued on. Rehana needed to speak to people at the Kurdish Red Crescent with messages and updates about the situation in Lanaco.

They were working out of a local council building on the main street and were easy to find.

The people at the Red Crescent were working with all the local Kurdish councils in the area to provide aid for the refugees. They were organising the distribution of all the food and bedding being sent in and matching it to all the pleas for help.

They had their work cut out.

The building was besieged. The doors were propped open to allow for the steady stream of people rushing in and out, and in the walled garden of the building hundreds of children sat and waited.

It was obvious that some of them were living here; there was a tarpaulin strung across a corner of the wall making a small triangular shelter and blankets and bedrolls were stacked underneath.

I wasn't sure if they were waiting for parents who were in the building or on their own. There were a few women with them – but only two or three.

As my gaze swept across them and I tried to do a quick headcount I suddenly heard my name being called.

"Dilvan. Dilvan Haco," called the little voice and I spun round to see my schoolfriend Silan* and her eight year old brother Sipan, pushing through the kids to reach me.

* PRONUNCIATION *Shee-Lan*

For a second the three of us just stood beaming at each other – we were so delighted. Then we hugged and held on to each other.

Striding into the building, Rehana called for me to wait for her in the garden. But when she saw Silan and her brother she raced over for a hug. "How long have you been here? Who are you with?" Rehana quizzed Silan, hugging her close.

But before Silan could answer one of the Red Crescent workers came to fetch Rehana for a meeting.

"Stay and catch up while I'm busy," said Rehana. "I'll come back for you here when I'm done," and with that she disappeared off inside the offices.

We carried on smiling and hugging each other, before Silan took my hand and pulled me to a quiet corner of the garden where we could sit and catch up.

Silan was the third of the three girls in my class at school. We'd been friends forever and I was really delighted to see her. She'd left the village before us to go and stay with family the other side of Lanaco – her dad thought it would be safer. He was wrong.

When we'd got over the shock of our reunion we both started talking at once. We had so many questions. So much had changed.

"You go first, Silan," I said. "Tell me everything that's happened since the last time I saw you."

She nodded and taking a deep breath she began.

"After we left the village we went to stay with my dad's family out south of Lanaco. My dad and his brothers all went with the YPG and all the women and children stayed in the family compound.

"It was all right at first – fun actually. All us cousins together, it was like being back in the village, wasn't it Sipan?"

He nodded and I realised that he hadn't spoken at all and as Silan continued, Sipan dropped his head and started to pick at the dirt under his fingernail.

"Yeah it was ok – at first. And then they came…"

"The ratmen?"

Silan nodded and grimaced and Sipan started to grind his teeth still intently picking his fingers.

"It was only a few of their patrols at first. But it was enough. They would stop in their trucks and set up checkpoints. They pulled people off buses and out of cars, dragged others out of their homes and shops. They were checking for anybody whose ID card didn't say Muslim at first. Christians were made to lie face down in the street and were shot in the back of the head. Even the children. They made everybody watch. It's not just the Christians – they don't like many Muslims either – just their own brand."

Gesturing to her brother, Sipan, she continued, "They took him off a bus. He and our cousin Feremez had been sent into town to get my grandad's heart medicine.

"They were on their way home when they were stopped at a checkpoint.

"A young girl on the bus was ordered to die because her hair was uncovered. She was only five. Her mum begged them to spare her and wouldn't let go of her daughter. Sipan, too, was ordered to be executed when they discovered he had a little copy of the Koran round his neck. They accused him of idolatry – for wearing it like a good luck charm. They're Muslims, Dilly, and yet they ordered him to die for worshipping the Koran…"

She trailed off – staring at me in disbelief at her own words.

I shook my head. But didn't speak. I've come to realise, lately, that words are not always enough to describe how you feel, particularly when things happen in front of you that are so shocking in their cruelty, so life-changing, so final, so pointless. There are no words in the world, certainly none that I know that would have helped at this point. So I said nothing and just waited as Silan was lost in her own thoughts for a moment and Sipan continued to gnaw at his nails.

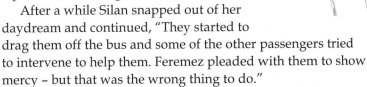

After a while Silan snapped out of her daydream and continued, "They started to drag them off the bus and some of the other passengers tried to intervene to help them. Feremez pleaded with them to show mercy – but that was the wrong thing to do."

Silan sighed and took a breath before continuing, her voice low and monotonous. "They decided to punish everyone for daring to question their authority so they ordered all of them off the bus and to line up facing a ditch at the side of the road."

I was watching Sipan as she spoke, goosebumps prickling my back like the cold fingers of the Dementors, crawling over my body, sucking the joy out of me.

"They opened fire on them with machine guns. As the firing started, Feremez's pulled Sipan in front of him," Silan swallowed hard. "He was only fourteen but he was very brave. Even at that moment he knew what was happening but he didn't cry, or run or beg for mercy and he saved Sipan," she said with pride, tears streaming down her face now.

Her voice cracked as she continued, "He was shot in the back and fell on top of Sipan into the ditch. No one noticed. Sipan was saved by his cousin. But he lay in the ditch under Feremez's dead body for two hours until they'd gone.

"Local people came to claim the bodies of their loved ones

for burial and that's when they discovered Sipan. His clothes stiff with the blood of the dead and he was rigid with fear.

"One of our neighbours recognised him and brought him home. He was black with the congealed blood of our cousin and his hair was sticking straight up into a bloody Mohican where it'd been trapped between all the bodies.

"Least they weren't beheaded," she muttered, almost to her self. "My mum says we should be glad about that – that at least it was quick.

"After we heard what had happened to Feremez and the others we left that night and came here.

"Sipan hasn't spoken since that day three weeks ago," she added.

We lapsed into silence again.

Somehow, knowing that most of my friends had suffered at the hands of the ratmen, united us and sharing the pain lessened it a little.

"What about you Dilly – how did you and Rehana turn up here all clean and fresh and smelling like daisies?" she questioned, nudging me with her elbow, wrinkling her nose and sniffing my hair.

"You two just come from the beauty parlour?"

"Kinda," I laughed and told them about Ipek's – even Sipan stopped grinding his teeth and picking his nails as I described the fabulous feast she'd served.

"Oooo you are soo lucky Dilvan Haco," exclaimed Silan. "We've been in the camp for three weeks, surviving on rice and beans – some days there's nothing.

"The people are nice. Lots of people bring food down and bedding. It's freezing at night. Kurds from all over the east of Turkey are starting to send supplies. That's why we're here. My mum's applying for another tent and rations for my aunt who arrived a couple of days ago. Where's your mum and sisters, Dilly? Are they in the offices too?"

I shook my head and Silan knew at once. "What happened, Dilly?"

"We were at my aunties' in the east of Lanaco when the enemy broke into the city two days ago.

"I was out getting supplies from the YPJ girls. They rounded up my mum and the girls and some others and put them on the back of a truck – but not Hira. One of them pinned her to the floor and was about to slit her throat when there was an airstrike."

"Oh," sobbed Silan, her hands flying to her face in shock.

"We don't know what happened to them after that. I'm hoping… I'm hoping…" the corners of my mouth dragged my bottom lip down to my chin and my face crumpled as I tried to voice the little flicker of hope that somehow, by some miracle she had survived.

The misery in my face was reflected in Silan's. "We're all hoping…" she nodded, reaching for my hand.

21. The Mudlings

Rehana still hadn't reappeared so Silan took me on a guided tour of the garden – introducing me to friends she'd made over the last few weeks.

It was more than two hours later that Rehana finally appeared out of the offices, together with Silan's mum.

They invited us back to the camp where they were staying – with other Rojava refugees in a field on the outskirts of Semikan and the five of us walked together up the street, chatting and catching up.

As we left the garden Rehana grabbed my wrist and said, "You'll never believe what just happened."

"What?"

"You won't believe it," she repeated.

"So just tell me then – what?"

I could see from the way she was trying to swallow a smile that it was obviously good news.

"What?" I pushed.

"Well you know after the fire fight the other day when the Americans arrived with General Zinar in the courtyard?"

I nodded.

"Well they tweeted a picture of me – and turns out I'm famous," she beamed.

"Famous? How?"

Rehana produced her phone and after a quick search handed it to me and there staring up from the screen smiling, arm raised

in a victory salute, was Rehana.

She was dressed in her YPJ fatigues and carrying her rifle and under her picture was written: 'Rehana has killed more than a hundred terrorists in Lanaco. RT and let's make her famous for her bravery'.

I looked up from the smiling girl on the screen to the grinning girl in front of me. "Go down... there's more," she urged.

Scrolling down, the post had been repeated more than 5,500 times in the past day and then picked up by a reporter who'd written a whole story about Rehana.

'Heroine of Lanaco: Kurdish Female Fighter Rehana Kills 100 Terrorists Single-Handedly' announced the headline.

It continued: 'A Kurdish female fighter has been hailed on social media for allegedly killing over one hundred terrorists single-handedly in the battle for Lanaco.'

The article went on to applaud the bravery of the YPJ and how the very survival of Lanaco depended upon them.

Other articles followed – 'Poster Girl of the YPJ', 'Lioness of Lanaco', 'Warrior Woman' – there were dozens of reports from all over the world.

All of them showing the picture of Rehana and recounting the bravery and determination of the Kurdish women warriors.

The picture said it all. Everything you might want to know about us shone from the photo of Rehana. Young, strong, Kurdish, happy, unafraid, ready to fight, beautiful...

It was odd seeing our situation reported from the outside but as I scrolled on I was bursting with pride.

Peering over my shoulder Silan read with me and by the end we were both a little awestruck by Rehana's new celebrity status.

Handing the phone back I threw my arms round her waist and squeezed her tight.

"I love you, Rehana," I whispered.

"Yeah, you too," she said squeezing me back. "Don't worry, I won't forget you when I'm famous," she joked.

"That is brilliant, Rehana," added Silan. "You're like a superstar now!"

"I know and the best of it is – it will absolutely choke Abdullah," laughed Rehana.

The three of us linked arms and carried on to the camp. On the way, Rehana explained that was why she was so long in the offices.

Her celebrity status was generating interest from newspapers and TV stations all round the world that were desperate for an interview with her.

It had been arranged for the next day and Rehana said she would have to leave me in Semikan while she went off to a secret location for filming.

"And I've got more good news," she added. "The general has sent a message saying your dad and brothers are due to appear before a judge on Wednesday or Thursday. It's just a formality so they should be released in time to arrive here by Friday at the latest."

Today was Sunday – so just five more days – five more days at most. It didn't seem that long to wait, but I was desperate to see them. I shoved those thoughts firmly out of my mind and decided, in the interests of being happy and hopeful, that I would just find ways to keep myself occupied until my dad got here then he would know what to do for the best.

With that settled we reached the refugee camp. It was on a field on the outskirts of Semikan. Row after row of blue plastic tents had been pitched on hardstanding. They were symmetrical and ordered and around and between them were the thousands of people who lived there. Children mainly, then women and old men, living in streets of mud.

It had rained earlier and the filthy water was collecting in pools where children had been playing in the dirt and ruts from car tyres – it was difficult to pick your way round the oozing slime that trickled between the tents.

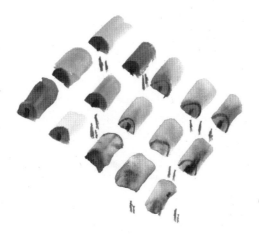

Sipan darted ahead leading the way to their tent which was several rows over to the back of the camp.

He was soon lost from sight in the heaving mass and it took us a while to catch up with him, carefully clinging to the little patches of dry ground, jumping over puddles and squeezing on to little dry islands to allow others to pass.

Silan's family now had two tents next to each other and the first we reached was the one newly allocated to her aunt.

Sweeping aside the flap we stepped inside to discover Silan's two aunts, their seven children, and her grandfather standing on the concrete floor of the tent.

They were standing in a line as if they were receiving guests at a wedding. Apart from the people, the tent was completely bare.

A baby was in a hammock slung from the tent poles and was being rocked to sleep by its mother, watched by the seemingly silent queue of relatives.

It was an uncomfortable glimpse of a cold, hard life but the sadness was soon dispelled by their delight at our visit.

Hugging and kissing and mashallahing took the next ten minutes, during which time we were ushered into the neighbouring tent where Silan and her family had been living for the last three weeks.

By comparison this tent was a palace. There were rugs on the floor, different coloured plastic chairs, and bedrolls stacked neatly in the corner with blankets and pillows on top. Three suitcases lay flat, one on top of the other, against a side wall, creating a funny little chest of drawers bulging with clothes.

At the front of the tent a large, red, plastic crate stood upturned on the floor. It served as a table-cum-work surface and through the criss-cross mesh you could see small bags of rice and tea and a few other essentials stored underneath along with some cooking utensils and matches.

Next to the crate was a gas bottle with a metal ring over the opening where you could balance a pan or kettle for cooking.

The chairs were reserved for Silan's grandparents and her pregnant aunt. The rest of us sat in a circle on the rug, and if it wasn't for the crinkling of the tent plastic in the wind, we could have been at home in the village.

Ever aware of her responsibilities as host, Silan's mother offered us tea. In the circumstances I thought it might be polite to refuse, but a glare from Rehana quickly reminded me that a refusal would be considered an insult to their hospitality, so I happily accepted.

I felt better when Rehana insisted they used the water from her canteen – as there wasn't a tap for miles.

But it took ages for the little gas flame to heat the pot of water to boiling.

Not that it mattered. No one had anywhere to go. Or anything to do. So we sat and chatted and waited for tea.

The conversation quickly became a roll-call of all the families in the village – house by house – swapping information about their fate or fortune.

All too often, we learnt the fate was death – fortune was a tent in a Turkish refugee camp and it was good to hear of many of our friends who had been fortunate enough to become refugees.

It might not seem so, but take it from me, there's a lot to be said for being safe.

Suddenly the flap of the tent flew open and what I can only describe as Mudlings, rolled in. Caked in mud and quarrelling, straw and scrud clinging to their clothes and poking from matted locks, they tumbled into the tent.

They were entirely brown from top to toe with a flaking crust which crumbled and swirled about them. Just their big brown eyes shone out of the swamp that enveloped them.

Despite the camouflage I knew them instantly. They were Silan's youngest sisters, Rozerin and Nupel, playmates of Hira's from the village.

Pushing and shoving and bleating they stumbled to a halt in front of us.

At three, Rozi was the older of the two. As the dust cloud settled around her I could distinguish mud-caked flip-flops, jeans rolled up at the ankle so they didn't trail in the dirt and a roll-neck jumper that, I think, was originally pink.

Her sister, Nupel, was two and her usually crazy curls were

123

stuck flat to her head with a big dollop of mud.

It was hard to tell where her flip-flops ended and her feet started or where her tracksuit bottoms reached as, from her stout little knees down, she was entirely cased in a crust of mud similar to one of our sheep.

The crust, although unbroken, thinned over the rest of her body and I could make out a Teletubbies picture on her sweatshirt.

Realising they held the floor, the Mudlings hesitated for a moment before Nupel burst out in indignation. Pointing at her sister with one hand and stretching out her sweatshirt with the other, she yelled, "She… she… she done got mud on my top," pointing at a wet patch on her jumper.

"She done it on mine own self! She… she…" she continued to scream, pointing at Rozi in fury, who, for her part stood as still as a lump of mud while she was accused – her existence only betrayed when she grimaced and rolled her eyes at the end of her sister's tirade.

We collapsed laughing and Nupel's foot stamping fury only made it funnier. We laughed until we couldn't breathe, tears streaming down our faces.

At one point Silan's grandad wheezed that he hadn't laughed that much since his wife had a fish swim up her jumper on a village outing to the river – a much loved Rojava yarn that had us laughing even longer until Silan's aunt begged us to stop before she gave birth on the spot – and the baby wasn't due for months.

When the laughter subsided and Rozi and Nupel had been pacified by a lollipop each from Rehana's secret supply it was time to go.

The night was drawing in and the cold started to nip at my fingers and my nose. I was glad to be going back to Ipek's with her electric fire.

Before we left, I promised Silan that I'd come and see her the next day while Rehana was doing her interviews and we agreed to meet up at the Red Cross office in the morning.

As we reached the entrance to the camp, Yahya pulled up in his car and offered us a lift.

He jumped out to open the door for Rehana and, making a mock bow, he said, "A coach for the heroine of Lanaco."

For dinner that night Ipek had surpassed herself, making Isli Kofte; little suet dumplings stuffed with savoury mince, and my very favourite. They were sticky and satisfying and served with a simple salad of lettuce and cucumber dressed with lemon juice and pomegranate vinegar.

The bitter-sweet, crisp salad and the little savoury parcels were the perfect combination and after we'd cleared up I spent an hour updating my diary with the rest and reunions we'd enjoyed since reaching Semikan.

22. SATELLITES AND STARS

The next morning we were both up bright and early – Rehana getting ready to be a star and me to meet Silan and while away another day waiting for my dad.

We met in the garden of the Red Cross office and waited for Rehana to find out what was happening.

It wasn't long before she returned.

"I have to go away overnight," she said. Then drawing me to a quiet spot she continued, "Listen, there's a top level meeting taking place tomorrow between our command and the Americans. The Americans have a TV crew with them, filming for a documentary about the situation in Lanaco.

"General Zinar has agreed to let them talk to me. They want a personal account and what with my new celebrity status," she grinned… "they think I'd be a great spokesman for the Kurds. General Zinar said there's a lot riding on this. He said we need the American people to understand our situation. He thinks I can help to make that happen."

She looked excited at the prospect of doing something positive for our cause and I was delighted for her. She deserved it.

"It means leaving you here for two days, but the general said Ercan's coming today and he can look after you 'til I get back. OK?"

I happily agreed. I liked Ercan and it would be a chance to find out if he'd heard anything from Jake or Richard about the satellite pictures that might tell me what happened to my mum and sisters.

I hugged her and wished her luck before waving her off in a convoy of trucks to continue our Kurdish crusade.

The trucks were hardly out of sight before Yahya pulled up outside the courtyard with the familiar crates I'd seen in the tunnel piled in the back of the truck he was driving. He'd clearly been on another supply run to the border and in the passenger seat was Ercan.

He bounded out of the truck to greet me.

"Isn't it great about Rehana?" he said as he hugged me. "Where is she – our poster girl?"

"You just missed her – she's off to continue her crusade. A celebrity mission for the general…"

"And that's why I'm here – to babysit you 'til she gets back," smiled Ercan, ruffling my hair. "So no getting into trouble while she's away – the general will roast me alive. OK? Promise?"

"I promise – anyway my dad will be back on Friday."

"Really? That's great news – we could do with him and your brothers in Lanaco," said Ercan.

"Look, Dilly, I put a call in to Jake and asked about those satellite pictures. I told him I was coming to see you today.

"He sent a message and said he's got news. He's arranged a skype call with me at 11am – which is in forty minutes," he said checking his watch. "Let's get inside and set the wi-fi up so we're ready."

"Can Silan come?" I asked – gesturing to my friend.

"I don't see why not," said Ercan. "Don't suppose you've got anything better to do," he smiled at Silan who laughed and shook her head.

We followed Ercan into the building which, as usual, was teeming with people and set off up the stairs.

It was a four storey building and there were throngs of people spread up the stairs over the first two floors, but as we climbed to the third floor it started to thin out and right at the top there were only a few people working on computers in one office.

Pushing open the door to another empty office, Ercan flicked the lights on and ushered us inside.

Silan and I sat and watched as he produced a laptop and charger from his bag and set it up on a desk.

We fetched three chairs while Ercan plugged the computer in and switched it on.

He was soon connected to a roaming wi-fi signal – but I didn't really understand what that meant.

He said that the Americans had boosted the wi-fi signal all along the Syrian/Turkish border so they could watch and listen to everything that was happening. He said they shared the wi-fi with us and it meant we could all keep in touch easily and send big files and video clips quickly.

Ercan was a bit of a geek and he obviously thrived on all the computer gadgetry and techno jargon.

I sensed he was relishing the opportunity of working with the Americans – sharing top secret information on a secret mission. Even if the mission was just to find out what had happened to my mum and sisters and was not essential to the war effort, it still meant that Ercan could forge new links with the Americans and glean more codes and contacts.

Even though it was a labour of love for Ercan, he knew it was life-changing for me and his running commentary on the technicalities of the task kept me from giving in to the terror of what the next hour might reveal.

We were set up, ready and waiting for Jake's call by 10.45am – then we just sat. Ercan and Silan did try to make conversation but I was too distracted.

Not knowing what had happened to them was torture – but

at least it brought with it the hope that somehow they might have escaped.

What if I were about to discover something worse? What if they were all… stop it. Stop it. STOP IT. I was shouting at myself in my head. Even thinking something bad might have happened felt like a betrayal – like tempting fate. I shoved those thoughts firmly away. I focused on my new motto: Have hope, have hope, have hope, have hope.

I was repeating it like a mantra in my head and picturing the smiling face of Zelal in her tractor on the border, then my mum in our garden, me and Elif racing the dog kart, Hira…

Thoughts and pictures tumbled through my mind whilst at the same time praying for good news.

I had already offered God everything I could think of if he would spare my mum and sisters. But why would God be swayed by my promises to work harder and not to lie, to try and be better…

And then it dawned on me and closing my eyes I rested my chin on my hands and prayed, "Dear God – if you could, in your brilliance, find a way to spare my mum and sisters, I promise, I absolutely swear that I will write it all down in my diary and then I will show it as proof that you saved them because they're good and because you can and because it would be good for people to see you're not on the side of the ratmen – whatever they say – I promise. Please. God. Thank you." And then the computer started to ring.

It took three attempts before we got a connection but finally we were looking at the smiling face of Jake.

"Hey Ercan, Dilly – good to see you," he shouted over the blat-blat-blat of rapid gun fire in the background.

"Look I can't talk – it's game-on here," he gestured behind him with one hand as the sound of mortar shells deafened us all and Jake's camera wobbled and lines of interference distorted the picture.

My heart was in my mouth – fearing we were going to lose connection. And then he was back – grinning and letting out a relieved whistle, "That was close." Other than 'Hello' I didn't really understand what he was saying but I got the picture.

Fortunately Ercan's English was much better than mine and Jake explained to him, "I've sent a message to you and Rehana. Understand?"

"Yes, yes, I understand," nodded Ercan.

"You read it first, Ercan, might be too much for Dilly to cope with on her own."

Ercan nodded and said, "It's OK, Jake. Her dad and brothers are due back here in a few days."

"Ah, that's great news – I'm delighted," said Jake.

And turning to me, Jake said, "Dilly, it's good news," he beamed. I had no idea what it meant, but the smile on his face and the thumbs up he was giving me were unmistakable.

I rewarded him with one of my happiest most grateful smiles and a thumbs up back – as did Silan.

"Sank yu," I shouted – remembering English from school as another almighty boom finally broke the connection with Jake.

23. My MUDLINGS!

Ercan ushered us out of the room as he read the message that Jake had sent and it was at least fifteen more minutes before we heard the 'good news'.

The waiting was unbearable and made me itch. Silan suggested we spend the time reciting prayers and passages from the Koran. She was a lot more devout than me but remembering that only minutes earlier I had promised God to be the very best I could manage, I readily agreed.

She picked a good one to start – a prayer for those in need, raising our hands to the heavens, we began: "Elhamdulillahille-zi afani mimma ibte-lake bihi ve feddaleni ala kesirin mimmen haleka tafdila…"

And so it was that Ercan discovered us chanting prayers as if our very lives depended on it – when he finally called us back in.

Ercan stood, smiling at our piety, as we finished the last prayer, and we all chorused "Amin" together.

Then beckoning me with his finger, he said, "I've got something to show you, Dilly."

We followed him back into the room. He sat on one side of the desk with the laptop facing him and indicated we should sit down opposite him.

No one spoke, and after a minute Ercan

turned the screen round to face me.

It was a grainy, black and white picture of a piece of wasteland taken from the sky… and there, in the corner, small but unmistakable, standing behind a big metal bin were my sisters.

Both of them. Together. Holding hands. Hira's face upturned to Elif's as if they were talking. They were as filthy as the Mudlings – but they were alive and I wept with relief and joy.

Hugging me and wiping my tears on her sleeve, Silan was asking all the questions that I was too overwhelmed to voice.

"Where are they? Where was this taken? When? Are there more?"

I couldn't peel my eyes away from the screen. Hira's little pink sprigged dress, Elif's curls. I touched their faces with my finger as I listened to Ercan explain.

"OK. This is a picture from an American satellite. It's one of the images that Richard requested and was taken four hours after the airstrike.

"Somehow, God only knows, they survived.

"This picture was taken below the square where you last saw them.

"And before you ask, yes there are more and there's more

information that Jake has sent in a message but for now be glad they're alive and let's make a plan when your dad arrives. OK?"

I was a bit dazed. In shock I think. But the prospect of waiting four days to rescue my sisters snapped me out of it.

"Whaaat? You can't do that Ercan. You can't just leave them – two tiny girls in a war zone. We have to go NOW. NooooooW," I screamed banging my fist on the table.

"And that's why Jake said not to show you everything. Look Dilvan – there's more at stake here than you realise.

"You can't have missed all the shelling and firing that's going on." I shook my head. The gunfire and airstrikes were as common as birdsong these days.

"There's a major battle underway for Lanaco right now. You gotta know that Dilly. We are stretched beyond our limits and we can't fail. Imagine what would happen to all those people at the border, everyone left in Lanaco – they would all be massacred.

"The girls have survived this far. But we don't know exactly where they are now. It's going to need your dad and brothers to mount a search for them. We'll all help – you know that – but right now we have to win this battle otherwise no one will survive.

"Try to be glad for small mercies, Dilly, the girls are alive – be glad and keep praying and let us work on rescuing them. OK?"

What could I say? What could I do? I needed their help and the Americans. Without it I wouldn't even know the girls were alive – but for how much longer? The pair of them, hand in hand skipping through a war zone. What if the ratmen found them again before we did? That would be too cruel.

My mind was racing. Ercan was resolute. He had neither the power nor the authority to do more than wait with me 'til my dad returned – but what if it was too late?

I stared at the picture of my sisters and tried to burn the image of their faces into my mind. I closed my eyes briefly, then looked again at the screen. It was impossible to tell where it was. My eyes darted round the screen to see if I'd missed any discernible features.

Nothing. I noticed that it was a message sent by email to Ercan from Jake and that he also sent it to Rehana – and suddenly a little flicker of inspiration came to me like a hot flush.

I glanced at Ercan and Silan to see if they noticed – but they were both intently staring at the screen too.

Sighing loudly I kissed my finger tips and touched them to my sisters on the screen. Together we said another prayer to keep them safe, "Bismillah ar-rahmen ar-rahim…" and realising my prayers were being answered I found renewed faith and strength.

Finally Ercan gently closed the computer.

"I still have some more stuff to do here for a while. Could you two wait for me in the garden 'til I'm done?"

Nodding in agreement I raced down the stairs with Silan hot on my heels.

24. CAFÉS AND CONSPIRACIES

I didn't stop until I got to the entrance – then grabbing Silan's shoulders I said, "We have to get to an internet café. Is there one in Semikan?"

"There's three," she grinned. "Why, what are you planning, Dilly?"

"We don't have long. Quick. I'll tell you when we get there."

Silan didn't need telling twice. She set off at a run and I was on her heels as she threaded in and out of all the Fugees and the folk on the street.

No one paid any attention to us and in a couple of minutes we'd reached the door of a dingy internet cafe.

"What are we doing?" questioned Silan.

"Look – Silan – that message and everything else in it that we didn't see was sent to Ercan and Rehana."

She nodded as I continued. "Well I know Rehana's password so I'm going to take a look."

A flicker of consternation reached her eyes but was quickly dismissed as she recognised the magnitude of the situation.

"OK, but we need money," she said pointing at a sign in the window that said it was four Turkish Lira for an hour of internet use.

Struggling to force my hand into the pocket of my jeans I produced a twenty Turkish Lira note. "Rehana gave it to me in case of emergency."

"Well this is definitely an emergency," confirmed Silan,

swiping the note from my hand and walking into the café.

The man in charge didn't look more than seventeen. He had a face full of spots and was so engrossed in his own screen that he barely looked at us as we entered.

"We'd like to use a computer please," Silan said, showing him my money.

"Fine, any one you want. You pay at the end – for the time – OK?"

We picked a quiet booth at the back of the café. There were a couple of local schoolboys gathered round another screen playing a fighting game.

Silan dragged up a chair next to me. And with a little conspiratorial nudge – we began.

Internet Explorer, hotmail sign-in, rehana85@hotmail.com, password azadiyakurdistan – free Kurdistan of course – if I hadn't known it I could have guessed it!

And after watching the little circle spin round for a few seconds – we were in.

I felt a little guilty at snooping – but I quickly got over it. I wasn't going to pry on anything else – just the pictures of my sisters – Rehana would understand.

There were a couple of unread emails – and there it was – sent from Jake this morning. I scrolled down and clicked on it.

It was a message with an attachment. Opening it we saw that the message was written to Ercan and Rehana from Jake but had been translated into Kurdish for them (and happily us) to understand. It read:

Hi guys,

I hope this message finds you both well and heading to victory. Here are the satellite pictures that Richard requested.

We have satellites and drones over Lanaco filming constantly and have miraculously managed to spot the girls. Hira is clearly identifiable from that picture of her with the knife to her throat and we believe the other child to be Elif, from Dilvan's description of what she was wearing – but this needs to be confirmed.

Having picked up that first image from Friday we have trawled images taken over the next sixty hours to nightfall Sunday and have discovered other shots of the girls.

Tracking the coordinates of the images through GPS they seem to be making their way out east of Lanaco.

Monitoring their route we can see that they are only travelling when the coast is clear and must be hiding at other times. How smart they are!

The last image was recorded just before nightfall yesterday, Sunday. Further images have not yet been uploaded so we cannot be sure of their exact whereabouts at this time.

We will keep monitoring the images with the intention of assisting a rescue with Nuri and his boys when they return. For now command are overwhelmed by the ongoing battle for Lanaco and unable to divert any manpower or resources. My fear is that the girls are heading towards the advancing enemy and I'm not sure how much time we have left to wait…

That last sentence made my blood run cold. I had known, since the second I saw my sisters alive, that I would do anything I could to save them – and it was clear we had no time to lose – despite anything Ercan said.

It is probably not a good idea to show all the pictures to Dilvan in case she decides to take matters into her own hands and mount a lone rescue mission. (Too late Jake!)

Nuri won't thank any of us for losing his third daughter when the first two are already in such a dreadfully precarious situation.

Time is of the essence. We are currently preparing the latest data on enemy movements and hope to outline a safe corridor for rescue when we have a clear idea where the girls are. Until then – stay safe – Jake.

We finished reading at the same time and Silan raised her eyebrows at me. I said nothing and clicked on the attachment.

25. ELIF & HIRA'S journey

Clicking the attachment opened a camera roll of dozens of pictures – although some were just the same shot, one taken from a distance and the next a close-up of the girls.

The first set was filmed during the airstrike. Smoke and dust billowed up from the frame but I could still make out the square where I had watched Hira pinned to the floor.

Date and time stamps showed the shots were taken in bursts for twenty minutes after the airstrike.

Opening the pictures, one after the other, I could make out the chaos in the square. The truck with my mother and sister on it was in the corner of the frame.

The smirking ratman is no longer bent over Hira but bent at the waist and blurry – as if he were running. By the look on Hira's face she's still screaming and very much alive.

I cursed myself. If I'd just waited a moment longer I wouldn't have been blown off that ridge and knocked unconscious myself by the airstrike. If only I'd waited another second – I could have watched the ratman flee and then darted in to scoop up my sobbing sister.

I was furious with myself.

The next picture was the same scene – enlarged even further so the picture was grainy but it was clear enough. It focused on the truck holding the women including my mum and sister.

The ratmen were fleeing to the truck to escape the American onslaught – but as they crowded onto one side they didn't

139

notice my sister, Elif, dangling
by her arm on the other, as my
mum quickly dropped her to the
ground.

In the next picture the truck
was disappearing in a cloud of dust
– but in the foreground I could clearly
see Elif, arms outstretched, running to
Hira who is still lying screaming on the floor.
I stared at that picture for a while. Anyone
else looking at it would see the chaos in Lanaco. The horror of
terrified children caught in the middle of an airstrike, but for
me it was heart-warming. I finally knew how Hira had been
spared. I took comfort from knowing that she would not have
realised what was happening and although she had been
terrified and traumatised, this picture told me that she was
soon wrapped in the loving and protective arms of her big
sister, that her tears would be dried and she would be kissed
and comforted until she felt better. It was, by no means a happy
picture, but it gladdened my heart.

The next shot was taken several hours later
and was the one of the girls by the bins that Ercan
had shown me earlier, and the wider image
showed exactly where they were – heading back
out of Lanaco. Despite the bombing and the debris
I recognised where they were – and my pulse
quickened as I realised where they were heading.

Date and time stamps on the shot showed
it was midday on Friday.

At first I thought they were heading to my
aunties' – which would mean one phone call
could send Kurdish soldiers round to find them.

140

But, opening the next picture I realised, with a sinking heart, that Elif had gone past my aunties'. I guessed she was too terrified to return to the house where they'd been seized.

The picture was taken on Saturday and this time it picked up the girls alone on a dusty track. At first it was hard to spot them, even in the close-up. They were the same colour as the track they were travelling on and their hair was like nests of straw. They must have slept or hidden in a bush or haystack – whatever the cause it was making them hard to spot and I was grateful for their camouflage.

The close-up showed the pair of them. They were walking hand in hand and Elif was looking back over her shoulder. She might only be six – but she clearly had her wits about her and was relishing the role of being in charge.

Zooming out to an aerial shot we could just about make out the little bushy dots on the path – they were heading towards the rising sun in the distance and instantly Silan and I knew where they were heading. They were going home. Home to Rojava.

"They're going home," said Silan.

"Yes," I agreed. "I don't suppose it would have been a difficult decision. Aside from my aunties', Rojava is the only place Elif knows – she didn't want to leave in the first place and moaned every day to go back.

"I reckon she was delighted to get the chance. It wouldn't have taken much to persuade Hira to walk either – I bet Elif just mentioned Xena and Xabur and Hira would be off at a trot as fast as her chubby little legs would carry her."

Silan laughed and nodded.

There were only a few more images left. We clicked on the next one. It was later and Elif was carrying Hira now. There was a grim determination on her face as she battled under the weight of her stocky sister labouring up the hill towards the village.

The last pictures were taken just yesterday, and they took my breath away. I clicked on the first image and there in front of me were the girls – laughing at each other – perched on the cliff top behind our house, their arms wrapped around Xena and Xabur.

My heart soared. They'd made it. Against all the odds. They'd escaped the clutches of the ratmen and wandered through a war zone. Hira, with her head firmly attached to her shoulders, defying and dispelling the gruesome memory of her screaming with the jagged little blade at her throat. The image that had haunted me since I last saw them.

Here she was. Laughing at her sister, her arm around Xena, the dogs dirtier and rangier than I remembered them, but wonderful to see them reunited. Safe.

That one picture told me a hundred things. Firstly that they were safe and alive, although clearly much stronger than I had realised. I marvelled at Elif's ability to guide her sister home, remembering a route she'd only travelled twice before while with adults.

I knew that they had access to food, water and shelter in our home and months of relentlessly playing mummies and babies reassured me that Elif was more than capable of feeding, washing and putting her baby sister to bed.

I was transfixed by the picture of the two of them. Sand-coloured children. They were children of this land and they were happy to be home.

A stifled sob and a sniff startled me back into the present and the fact that Silan was sobbing beside me.

I would be lying if I didn't admit that I, too, had tears streaming down my face and had, I now realised, been quietly crying as I worked my way through the photos of my sisters.

But seeing Silan's swollen, tear-stained face was less surprising than hearing her say, "These are happy tears, Dilly. Look at them. The pair of them. They're so happy. So happy to be home," she trembled.

And she was right. They were happy. It seems such a simple thing. But it's what we all wanted – to be at home and happy.

This picture was my 'Patronus Charm' against the Dementors and I sat and stared and sucked joy from it for ages and I felt peace for the first time in weeks.

26. The Advance of the RATMEN

Sadly that peace was short-lived.

I clicked to enlarge the last remaining frame. It was the wider shot of the girls on the cliff. They were just tiny dots now barely distinguishable in a grainy picture which panned out wide across the valley below our house.

It took me a moment to get my bearings and I had to squint to make out the specks on the cliff top.

Letting my eye stray across the screen I took in the meander of the river as it worked its way down the hill, disappearing out of sight in parts then reappearing to snake its way through the valley.

I'd never seen my home from the sky before and it looked odd. But the more I focused the more things I recognised.

I could make out the roof of our house and my mum's orchard and vegetable garden and the track down to the market – just the track though, the rest of the village was out of shot.

The picture took in the girls on the cliff and then panned out across the valley and plains – the view I knew like the back of my hand.

It was where I'd stood with Rehana and virtually the whole village, singing farewell to my dad and brothers.

Familiarising myself with local landmarks my eyes greedily ate up the land across the valley racing towards the horizon – and then stopped short.

There in the distance, on the horizon, was an unmistakable,

straggly black line. A black stain seeping across the land.

It was the ratmen and they were heading straight to Rojava. Rojava and my little sisters, with only dogs to protect them.

My hand instinctively shot towards the screen trying to fend them off. I thought I would be sick.

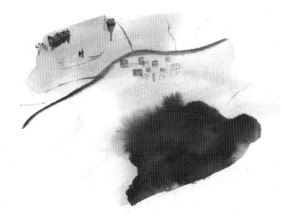

Silan saw it at the same time and we gaped at each other in horror. The happy tears suddenly burning our stiff and swollen cheeks.

"How far away are they?" asked Silan.

Checking the time on the two previous images showed the ratmen had hardly advanced in four hours.

For the time being they were being pinned down by American airstrikes and I took a moment to thank God for the Americans, again.

There was another small village between the spreading stain of death and Rojava.

I knew that the village was an hour's drive from our house so reckoned they were easily two hours away by car – and, it appeared, they were walking.

"Assuming they set off again," I said.

"And I've heard they're mainly travelling at night to avoid the American warplanes," Silan volunteered positively.

"Well then it would easily take them three nights to reach Rojava.

"The pictures were taken last night – so that means they could reach the village by Wednesday. That's the day after tomorrow, Silan and two days before my dad even gets here. They can't wait that long. I can't wait that long. We have to do something and we have to do it now," I wailed at her.

Seeing my desperation, Silan took charge of the immediate situation.

"Right now we have to get back to the garden before Ercan realises we're missing," she said. "We'll have plenty of time to make a plan then," she added.

I liked her use of the word 'plan'. It sounded positive, so reluctantly I logged out of Rehana's email as Silan paid the spotty boy for the half hour we'd been sat sobbing at a screen in his café.

I don't know what we looked like, and I don't really care. It was the best two lira – however much that is in real money – that I've ever spent.

Running back to the garden I already knew what I had to do. I had to go and get the girls myself and bring them here. If I was quick I could reach them and be back under the border before the ratmen got to Rojava. Reaching the garden we slumped in a quiet corner to plan.

It didn't take us long to thrash out a brilliant rescue mission. We kept it simple, if daring, and had rehearsed and improved it several times before Ercan even reappeared from the building looking for me.

27. Plots, Plans and Rice Pudding

Plotting and planning and looking at pictures had taken up virtually the whole day. The sun was disappearing across to the other side of Turkey.

I'd already given Silan the money that was left and she was to initiate stage one of the plan.

"Hey girls," called Ercan as he strode out of the building and across the garden towards us. "Sorry I've been so long."

"No problem," we chorused.

"We've been testing each other on maths and teaching tables to some of the little kids..." I lied.

Once I'd committed to a rescue plan I'd known that I was going to have to lie and deceive some of the nicest and kindest people that I'd met.

I wasn't proud of it – but the only thing that mattered was reaching my sisters and saving them and I was willing to do whatever it took.

I'd persuaded Silan that when I arrived back with the girls, everyone would be so delighted that they'd forget all the little lies we'd told.

She hadn't, even for a moment, tried to talk me out of going as she knew there was no point. At first she campaigned to come with me, until I told her about the minefield and, forced to be cruel to be kind, told her she'd be more of a hindrance than a help.

"Look Silan, I picked my way through that minefield once

and I can do it again – but it'll be dark and I can't guide you across. There's no point in you coming just to keep me company and then get yourself blown up. Imagine the trouble I'd be in then? Anyway – I'll be much quicker on my own and time is the most important thing.

"I just need to get there and get back with the girls – OK? I love you for volunteering but I really need you to help me here."

I think the minefield story did the trick. I didn't tell her that we'd crossed linked in a line or that there was quite a clear path.

I didn't want the responsibility of risking her life – when there was really no need.

Reluctantly she gave in and agreed to be second in command, based in Semikan. With that settled the other details came together quite easily.

Silan was going to use the rest of the money to go and buy a torch for me to use. Then she was going back to the camp to find her cousin. He'd made friends with a local boy who had a scooter. She said we could borrow it for the price of some petrol.

Everything was organised, so when Ercan came to collect me, we said a cheery goodbye and made fake plans to meet each other in the morning at the camp.

As she hugged me she whispered, "See you tonight," and the butterflies in my tummy fluttered up to my throat. I felt excited and sick at the prospect.

Yahya was waiting for us outside in the truck with the crates on.

"What are the crates for?" I asked him as I slid onto the passenger seat to make room for Ercan.

"It's all different stuff," he replied. "Anything from weapons and ammo to medicine, bandages and food. All the supplies for our forces in Lanaco."

I nodded and filed the information away in case I needed it later.

On the drive, Yahya asked Ercan if he could help update the computer they were using to coordinate all the supplies being sent from other Kurdish councils in Turkey.

"Yeah, of course, no problem – but I reckon it'll have to be tonight. I've got meetings all day tomorrow and I'm not sure how much longer I'm going to be here."

I held my breath. The prospect of the pair of them going out was better than I could have hoped. It would only leave Ipek – and being pregnant she was always tired and nodding off – she'd be delighted if I suggested an early night.

"Fine by me," agreed Yahya. "The sooner the damn thing's fixed the better. We'll go straight to the warehouse office after we've eaten."

It was music to my ears.

I felt a little guilty when I saw how tired Ipek did look when she opened the door. But nothing was going to deter me and an early night really would be good for her.

She'd stuffed peppers and vine leaves, tomatoes and aubergines with savoury rice for dinner and the smell from the kitchen made my mouth water.

As soon as we arrived Yahya told her that they would be leaving again after dinner.

"It's all ready – sit down and I'll bring it now if you're in a rush," said Ipek as she bustled into the kitchen to fetch the floor cloth and cutlery.

The plate of stuffed veggies looked like a work of art. Ipek must have spent hours, carefully slicing the tops off the tomatoes and peppers and hollowing out the insides. She mixed the contents with onions and savoury rice and minced meat that she'd prepared and carefully spooned back inside to cook.

The result was delicious, just like my mum's.

I thought about her as I ate. She was the only one of my family still missing. What kind of hell must she be in? Enslaved by the ratmen. Not knowing the fate of any of her children and powerless to help them. I knew better than to dwell on such miserable thoughts.

My mum might not be here or able to help, but I was. I would get the girls and when my dad and brothers returned they could concentrate on rescuing my mum.

"No time for tears, Dilly," I could hear her voice in my head. My mum was a strong and capable woman and I reckon she would have given her blessing to my rescue mission.

"You're quiet tonight, Dilly," Ipek's voice shattered my daydream. "You OK sweetheart? Missing Rehana?" she asked, raising her hand to my forehead to check if I had a temperature. I nodded and seized the chance to put the next stage of the plan into action.

"I'm just tired. I think the last few days have finally caught up with me," I said, stifling a yawn.

"Well not too tired for pudding, I hope," exclaimed Ipek. "I've made rice pudding specially for you."

"Ooo no definitely not too tired for pudding," I agreed. "But I wouldn't mind an early night if that's ok?"

"That's a great idea," agreed Ipek.

Pudding was a triumph. Little bowls of the creamy sweetened milk pudding topped with a dollop of apricot purée. It was delicious.

Yahya and Ercan left soon afterwards and we chatted as I helped Ipek to clear up.

I felt the most guilty at betraying Ipek's kindness and resolved to make amends.

Laying out my bedroll in the sitting room, I checked the

time on the TV. It was only 8.30pm so I had hours left to wait.

"I think I'll update my diary," I told Ipek. "That should send me to sleep in a second."

"OK, sweetheart, I'm just going to put some washing on and then that's me. I can't wait to put my feet up. I'll see you in the morning."

She was gone and I listened to her busying herself with the laundry before opening my diary and carefully tearing off half of one of my precious blank pages.

I used it to write a note to Ipek, thanking her for all she'd done for me and explaining about my sisters and the peril they were facing. I apologised for betraying her trust and hoped that she'd understand.

I signed it with love and kisses and then added, "PS Make a big breakfast – I'll be back with my sisters! – Inshallah."

I folded the note in half and wrote Ipek's name on it.

It was after nine now and my butterflies felt friskier than ever. I decided to use the time to update my diary with today's revelations and to calm the butterflies that had clearly donned clogs now to dance around my insides and fill me with fear and trepidation about the night ahead.

Recalling the pictures of my sisters on their traipse home and reunited with the dogs calmed my churning tummy and by the time I'd finished it was 10.38pm and not much longer to wait.

Feigning a trip to the toilet I took the chance to listen at Ipek's door. It was left slightly ajar for Yahya and through the crack I could hear her regular peaceful breathing. The house was quiet, except for the occasional drip from the tap in the kitchen.

Slipping back into the sitting room I collected the bits I thought I might need for the rescue mission.

I put my diary into my small bag, along with a bottle of water, a bar of chocolate (in case of emergency) and Rehana's big hunting knife that she'd left in her rucksack in the corner of the room.

Peering out of the window I checked to see if Silan had arrived. The street was quiet, but not empty – the Fugees were always there.

No sign of Silan. I gnawed at my thumbnail. What if her cousin couldn't get the scooter? She'd been so confident earlier I hadn't questioned it, but now fears flooded my brain.

What if she couldn't slip away unnoticed? What if she'd crashed it? What if I had to run all the way to the border? It was only five minutes by car but probably a good five kilometres away. What if I stood here worrying so long that Yahya returned?

But as I stood agonising at the window I suddenly heard the put-put-put of an ancient scooter and standing on tiptoe, squashing my forehead to the pane, I spied Silan wobbling and shaking as she rattled towards me.

I was ready. I placed the note for Ipek on the side table, propped in front of her wedding photo so she would be sure to see it. Then I slipped back out of the door and across the hallway.

The door wouldn't be bolted 'til Yahya returned and locked up. I doubted he'd check on me – but just in case I bundled Rehana's rucksack and cushion up inside my blanket to make it look like I was sleeping.

Quietly, slowly I eased the handle down and cursed the click as the metal latch sprung free from the lock. I paused, holding my breath, waiting for the sound of stirring from Ipek's room – but it was silent.

Easing myself round the door I edged into the corridor and gently clicked it shut behind me. I ran swiftly down the stairs and out on to the street where Silan was waiting for me with the engine running. The put-put noise of the rickety old

scooter was starting to attract attention from the Fugees.

"Hurry up," hissed Silan. "I daren't turn it off – it's a bugger to start." I didn't need telling twice and hopped on the seat behind her.

We didn't speak until we'd cleared Semikan and were on the abandoned road to the border.

"Feel like I could be driving you to your death," Silan shouted back to me over her shoulder.

"Thanks!"

"No – it's just that my mum will murder me if you get caught."

"Well that's OK then – so if I don't see you back here – I'll see you in the afterlife!"

"Don't joke about that Dilvan Haco," Silan scolded.

Ten minutes later and Silan turned off the road onto the dirt track that led to the farmhouse with the entrance to the secret tunnel in the cellar.

There were still people milling around outside. They ignored us and we ignored them – pretty much.

Silan pulled up near the back of the house and I hopped off the bike and hugged her. Handing me the torch she showed me how it worked then hugged me hard.

"Good luck, Dilly."

"Thanks Silan, thanks for everything – I'll bring the girls to play with Rozi and Nupel when we get back," I beamed at her.

"You do that," she said, beaming back at me.

"OK, you know the plan – stay here, count to one hundred slowly and if I'm not back it means I'm in the tunnel and on my way!"

28. TRAPDOORS, TUNNELS and TREE ROOTS

I turned and entered the back door of the farmhouse which had been propped open with a brick.

The trapdoor was already open and men were coming up from the tunnel having just delivered more crates.

"You're going the wrong way, luv," joked one man as I passed him, heading down the steps.

"No you're all right, Uncle," I called back, using the traditional form of respectful greeting. "Yahya sent me to get something from one of the crates."

"You need a hand?" asked the old man.

"No, no I'm fine," I assured him. "Yahya needs me to get some medicine. I know where it is and it's not heavy. I'll be fine – but I better hurry – he'll be back for me in a moment."

The men seemed satisfied with my explanation and went back up to the kitchen of the farmhouse.

So far so good. The tunnel here was wide and well lit and I could see the crates all stacked up against the wall.

Automatically I darted over to them and pretended I was looking for one in particular. Glancing over my shoulder I checked to see if anyone was looking from the stairs up to the kitchen.

The trapdoor was still open and I could hear their voices echoing down to me in the tunnel – but no one was watching and as I reached the end of the line of crates I broke into a run.

I didn't stop until I reached the point where the tunnel narrowed. Pulling the torch from my bag I leant against the cold rock of the walls and turned it on.

It was a halogen beam and provided a strong white light. A thudding sound made me catch my breath until I realised it was my heart hammering against my ribs.

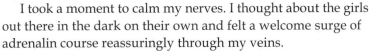

The butterflies in my stomach had morphed into bats swooping and swirling round my insides.

I took a moment to calm my nerves. I thought about the girls out there in the dark on their own and felt a welcome surge of adrenalin course reassuringly through my veins.

"Nothing to fear, nothing to fear, get the girls and get back," I told myself sternly and kept repeating this as I pushed on into the narrowing tunnel.

It was much slower-going here. With one hand tracing the wall of the tunnel I used the torch to pick out the ground in front of me.

It was one long channel that wound under the ground to Syria but after twenty minutes of walking I feared I'd gone wrong.

I ploughed on and just as a rising panic was threatening to get the better of me, I felt a cool breeze reach my face.

Just a little further and I was in the cavern staring up at the tree roots that shielded the opening above me.

And here I discovered the first flaw in my plan. Getting in had been easy. I'd just wriggled over the edge and dropped to the cave floor. Standing here staring up I realised that getting out would be another matter entirely.

The hole was in the centre of the cavern roof above me – but out of my reach by at least two metres.

Through it and the lattice of tree roots I could see the low white disc of a full moon. I counted my blessings and quickly extinguished my torch knowing its beam could give away the opening to the secret tunnel.

It took a moment for my eyes to adjust but the moon beams bounced off the cave floor and lit up the walls to reveal the impossibility of trying to scale the rock to reach the opening.

I would have had to climb upside down across the roof of the cave to reach it.

Tree roots seemed the best, actually only, option. I raked through a few until I found the thickest and yanked it hard a couple of times.

It held, so I dragged it to the side of the cave and started to inch my way up, pulling hand over hand on the tree root and climbing the wall with my feet.

It was painstaking but life in the village had prepared me well – climbing was a favourite pastime and employing all the skills I'd gleaned from my childhood I made steady progress away from the cavern floor and ever closer to the opening above.

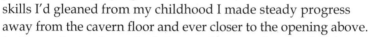

I was almost there. And then, as I swung the weight of my body and stretched out to reach the opening, the root snapped and slammed me into the wall of the cave before I crashed back to the floor.

I lay for a moment, wincing on the floor. I'd cracked my head and elbow on the wall and scraped my back and shin down the rock face.

It was stinging and throbbing but I didn't feel any real pain. Yet.

I gingerly sat up and had to wait another moment before my head stopped spinning.

Reaching for the torch, I covered the beam with my cupped hand and turned it on so I could peer at my leg. It was scraped and bleeding but I'd had worse.

Then, just as I flicked the torch off, I thought the beam glinted off something shiny in the corner of the cave.

Carefully switching it on again, I played the beam across the floor of the cave. There. In the corner behind more tree roots.

I crawled across the cavern floor to investigate.

It looked like a silver pole but when I reached it I realised it was a ladder.

Of course. I knew they used this tunnel both to get in and out of Syria. There had to be an easy way to reach the hole – if only I'd known.

Muttering curses, that I had often heard my brothers use, at my own stupidity, I wrestled the ladder free from where it was stashed behind the tree roots decorating the cave wall.

It was two ladders joined together with a spring clip. By releasing the clip, one side of the ladder slid forward and clicked into place – making one long ladder that could easily reach the opening above me.

Propping the bottom rung on a flat piece of the floor I wavered around for a moment before slamming the top of the ladder through the hole.

A little bit of jiggling and it was steady – an instant staircase to Syria.

29. Homeward Bound

Emerging out of the hole I took a moment to organise myself with my bag and my wounds and my thoughts.

I couldn't use the torch now – the light would signal to all and sundry for miles and the idea was to sneak in, get the girls and sneak back.

Happily the moonlight was silvery and bountiful. It silhouetted the trees and tracks that I needed to follow without shattering the comforting cloak of darkness that would shield me from view.

Perching on the edge of the rise my eyes bored through the gloom to pick out the start of the 'safe-track' across the minefield.

The earth was beaten and flattened by boots on the trusted strip through the furrowed field.

I've done it before – I can do it again, I told myself. But still I didn't move.

I couldn't work out whether to look ahead to the finish or down at my feet. It's funny how walking in a straight line can be really difficult when you overthink it.

I opted for a combination of the two – I looked down before I took a step and then ahead before I put my foot down. Arms either side for balance – like I was walking a tightrope.

It was slow-going to start – but after I stopped making such a meal of it – it got easier and faster. I exhaled when I heard my boot hit the reassuring crunch of the path and realised I'd been holding my breath across the field. I'd made it.

It was only a few short steps down the path to the top of

the track that I'd glimpsed the other night.

There was no cloud cover tonight and fingers of moonlight beckoned me to the turning. This was the road my dad and brothers had taken to Turkey. It led straight down to the valley then twisted up the hillside to the top of Rojava.

Dancing ahead of me like a child, the moonlight was already playing on the river – waiting for me to catch up.

I was grateful for the company of the bouncing beams that lit up the river like a silver snake, guiding me home.

I crunched on down the path, before breaking into a run. I guessed it was about five kilometres to the village – if I pressed on I could be there in the hour, the sooner the better.

To my right I could see Lanaco burning and hear the familiar song of gunfire and shells over the blacked out city. It was eerie. A ghost town – lit only by the flames of untended fires.

The rumbling thunder of a distant airstrike made my cheeks wobble and my ears pop.

I had no idea what the time was – but a familiar glow of pink on the horizon told me it would soon be sunrise and too dangerous to travel.

Running down to the valley floor was easy with the momentum of gravity. Reaching the lower plain my boots suddenly felt heavier but still I ran on towards my home and the sisters waiting there for me.

Climbing the hill to the village became a struggle. I'd run it many times before – but not after completing what felt like a marathon.

I slowed to walking, then stopped to let the spasm of a stitch pass. My mouth was sticky and I couldn't swallow or even spit. My water was a welcome treat. A couple of swigs and I was ready to run again – sprinting the last hundred metres to the top of the hill.

The little streak of pink on the horizon was widening to an orangey band as birdsong heralded the dawn. I peered into the distance – trying to make out the advancing line of ratmen I'd seen in the picture but it was still too dark.

Nearly there, nearly made it. I turned down the track to Rojava and round the bend to the front of our house. Everything exactly as I remembered but abandoned now.

Walking across the garden I glimpsed movement on the verandah. Squinting into the shadows I could make out the raised hackles of Xabur. He'd seen me – but hadn't made a sound. Xabur's instincts were herding and protecting and right now he was protecting a very important flock.

Dropping to one knee I called to him in a whisper, "Xabur – come boy – it's me." He bounded across the garden and knocked me over in delight, bouncing on the spot, licking and nuzzling.

Which of us was more delighted was hard to tell. It was a magical, if rushed, reunion. As soon as I'd hugged him I straightened up and asked, "Where are they boy? Where's the baby? Where's Elif? Xena? Show me…"

He knew what I was looking for and with a cursory glance behind me to make sure there were no unseen dangers he set off round to the back of the house with its elegant French windows.

Opening the door I followed Xabur inside and through to my parents' bedroom.

And there – curled up and fast asleep in the big bed – were Xena and both of my sisters. Leaping off the bed with delight, Xena woke Elif. Her curly head raised from slumber, a little groggy, she peered into the darkness.

Standing at the foot of the bed, I watched and smiled as her eyes slowly focused and bouncing straight from her knees she

160

was in my arms.

I held her and hugged her and kissed her and cried with her. We wept with relief and joy at our reunion.

"Dilly, Dilly," was all she could seem to say between sobs. And our sobbing woke Hira who stretched out her chubby little arms to me and then the three of us were just a tangle of tears and clasping each other, we collapsed onto the bed. Not much was said. This was a physical reunion. I traced their faces with my fingers and smoothed their hair. They, in turn, held my face and kissed me, wet slobbery, puckered-up smackers.

The terror and sheer exhaustion of everything that had happened had taken a dreadful toll on them both. They were tearful and trembling and overjoyed at the same time. Nothing mattered now. They were alive and any harm, any lingering nightmares could be kissed away in time.

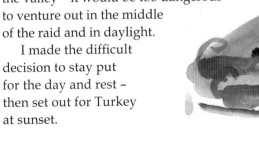

Settling back on the bed – with one of my sisters under each arm – I held them close and reassured them. I marvelled at their strength and bravery and told them, between kisses, about everything that had happened since we'd been torn apart.

With a sniffle and a final shivery spasm I realised Hira had fallen asleep in my arms and brave little Elif was struggling to keep her eyes open.

The airstrike was still raging across the valley – it would be too dangerous to venture out in the middle of the raid and in daylight.

I made the difficult decision to stay put for the day and rest – then set out for Turkey at sunset.

I wondered where our puppies were – Elif hadn't seen them. I hoped they were still running free up on the mountain and not venturing near the village like their loyal parents.

Resting my chin on Elif's head I said, "You're brilliant, Elif. Brilliant and brave."

"Cos I'm Kurdish," she smiled up at me.

"Yup, you're a warrior woman for sure," I said, squeezing her tight and smiling. "Sleep now – you'll need your strength for the journey."

She blinked her big brown eyes up at me once, the second time they stayed shut and she was asleep – and so was I.

30. Rehana to the RESCUE

Sleeping. Stretching. Scratching. Sleeping. Sleeping sisters.
Smell of dog. Sunshine stroking my cheek.

Senses creep upon me as I stir.

Dozing now.

Sunlight streaming through the windows. Sounds of my
mum bustling out in the kitchen. So familiar.

School. Must be time for school soon.

Snoozing. Drifting comfortably down again into the warm
embrace of sleep.

Sleeping. Stretching. Scratching. Sleeping. Sleeping sisters.
Smell of dog.

Sunshine stroking my cheek.

Senses creep upon me as I stir.

Someone stroking my cheek.

So familiar.

"Is it school-time, Mum?" I croaked.
Opening half an eye to smile, lazily at her…

"REHANA! REHANA?!"

Wide awake now. Upright. All
dreams dispelled like a burst bubble.

Head to toe in army fatigues and
swathed in ammo – it was Rehana
who'd been stroking my sleeping face.

Momentarily disorientated on
waking, my eyes darting round the

room, I realised it wasn't all a dream. I was at home. My sleeping sisters were next to me on my parents' bed, Xabur and Xena watching through the open door.

And there perched on the edge of the bed before me was… Rehana. I shook my head and widened my eyes in disbelief.

But it was her.

And from her gentle expression – albeit, slightly frowning, I knew I was forgiven for my recklessness and was saved.

Turning to look at my sleeping sisters the frown fell from Rehana's face and opening her arms to me she smiled.

I hugged her tight – overcome with relief. It's funny when you really have to be strong – you are. But the minute someone turns up to relieve you – you wilt like a plucked daisy and so I collapsed in her arms, burbling, "I'm sorry… I know I shouldn't have but that… it's… well my sisters and I saw the pictures and I knew where they were and then the ratmen and I couldn't wait and I couldn't reach you and they said my dad wouldn't get here for days and so I had no choice really I didn't I couldn't leave them not after Elif had been so strong I couldn't leave them to fall into the hands of the ratmen again not after they'd been sooo brave and escaped once and got home and I knew we didn't have any time and…"

"Yeah – I get it," said Rehana, hugging me back. "Why do you think I'm here?"

"'Cos Silan told you."

"Yes. I got back early this morning to find a distraught Ipek and defiant Silan waiting for me.

"Ah, Dilvan Haco," she sighed, ruffling my hair. "You did the right thing – I would have done the same." She hugged me tight to her – then, holding me away from her by my shoulders, she said, "But now we have to get out of here," and there was an urgency to her voice I hadn't heard before.

"Last night's airstrikes were trying to slow the advance of the caliphate, but still they come." She closed her eyes, shaking her head.

"When Silan told me this morning I came straight here. But they are here Dilly," she hissed.

"I saw them crossing the valley floor. We have to go – we can't let them find us." Our talking had woken Elif and her squeals of joy on seeing Rehana woke Hira.

Even the minutes we shared hugging and rejoicing seemed to stoke Reh's anxiety.

Where I come from there's a saying 'Keca Kurda' which is hard to explain. It actually means 'Kurdish girl' but to us it implies 'Warrior woman. Woman of honour. Kurdish heart'.

"Keca Kurda," breathed Rehana, in awe of Elif's epic journey and rescue of her sister. And I watched Elif swell with pride from the praise.

Kneeling to her level, Rehana spoke directly to Elif, woman to woman, "OK Elif – I know how strong and brave you are. I need you to stay strong for me now. You have to do what I say, when I say. This is what you have to do, Keca Kurda, to be a soldier of Kurdistan, OK?"

Elif nodded with a very serious face.

Sensing the urgency I whipped the girls into shape – sorting shoes and hair and a drink and a wee while Rehana slipped outside to check the coast was clear.

It wasn't.

Racing back to the verandah Rehana hissed, "Get the girls and come. NOW..." Reaching the verandah, Rehana scooped Hira into her arms, "Follow me, stay low and silent," she ordered.

"What is it Reh?" I stammered.

"They're here. In the village," she hissed. "We need to go."

We didn't need telling twice. I grabbed Elif's hand and

followed Rehana out of the back of the house towards the cliff edge.

Sliding onto the narrow path that led over the cliff top towards the caves I heard the sound of a truck coming up the track.

It was them. The stinking ratmen. In Rojava. As they rounded the bend past the market I caught a glimpse. It was an open-back white truck with a machine gun fixed in the back.

In true Dementor form, the sight of them made my blood run cold. There were two in the front and three more in the back, bearded, filthy and in Rojava.

I was rooted to the spot – in shock, so Rehana dragged me onto the path and between us we got the girls and the dogs into a cave and out of sight… for now.

31. Looking for a Way out...

We sat in the cave in silence. Staring at each other. Listening to the sounds echoing down to us from above.

The honeycomb network of caves that spread out under our village made sound bend and travel in peculiar ways.

But we were accustomed to this and used it to our advantage. Listening, placing them, counting, planning.

The bustling sound I'd mistaken for my mum in the kitchen this morning, turned out to be Rehana – who had taken the chance to swiftly prepare a picnic of fruit from the garden and biscuits and nuts from my mum's cupboards.

Sitting silently in the cave we shared a feast of nectarines and pomegranates, peaches and plums, biscuits and sunflower seeds.

We hardly spoke, but it dawned on me that Hira hadn't spoken at all.

"She's not spoken since Lanaco," Elif confirmed.

"I've had to do all the talking for the two of us," she boasted. "It's not been easy."

And I thought of Silan's brother, Sipan, who had also been struck dumb since his encounter with the ratmen.

Remembering the charm for encountering a Dementor I reached in my bag and grappled around for the chocolate bar I'd brought with me, in case of emergency.

Breaking off a chunk I popped it in Hira's mouth and the grin she gave me was reward in itself – although she still remained silent. Perhaps it would take a moment to work, I reasoned, handing the rest of the bar to Elif to share with our little sister.

This was one of the forbidden caves. The one with the hole that plunged and plummeted down to the river below.

The sound of the ratmen had moved away from the cliff top but we could still hear them in the village.

Reappearing from the back of the cave, Rehana said, "They're looting all the supplies from the market. I can hear them talking – but I think it's English." She looked puzzled.

"I don't get it. Britain's supposed to be a wonderful country. They give you money and a house even if you don't work. Why would anyone want to leave to come here and kill kids?"

I didn't have an answer. Shrugging, I said, "Perhaps it's just the horrid ones?"

Nodding, exasperated, Rehana added, "And there's something else – they've got hunting dogs with them. I heard them snarling and howling – sounds like a crazed pack."

British boys with hunting dogs!

I gaped in horror remembering what Ercan had told me in the courtyard. His words echoed in my head, "It was British and Tunisian boys that came to my village… they come up with the sickest forms of torture… they used shepherd dogs… they set them on the kids… they're starved and beaten…"

Was it possible? The same weird cult of killers now in Rojava.

The noose of fear that had been strangling me tightened a little further – I struggled to swallow – no matter – my mouth was dry and my cheeks were throbbing.

"I've heard about them, from Ercan," I told Rehana.

"Me too," she nodded. "We need to get away from here – fast." I wasn't arguing and she continued, "I need to work out our escape route. While they're busy at the market, you take the girls down to the bottom cave – the one below the river near the old track."

I knew the cave she meant and nodded.

"I'll scout out a route and then meet you there – we can get away from the village on the old track when I've worked out a safe route across the valley."

The old track was rarely used these days – it was a long, wide and wiggling way – but it was shielded by the overhanging cliff which would afford us some protection.

Putting her arm round my shoulder, Rehana walked me to the front of the cave – our backs to the girls who were passing the time cracking sunflower seeds between their teeth.

Unclipping a grenade from her belt she handed it to me. "In case of emergency," she said.

It was heavier than I imagined and cold to touch.

"You know how it works?" quizzed Rehana, and I shook my head.

"OK if you have to – if you have no other choice – don't let them take you alive. If it comes to that. If they reach the cave before me, then sit together with the girls, pull this pin and count to three, and I'll see you all in paradise."

That was grim. I felt the panic that had been coursing through me for days ratchet up a level.

Seeing my face, Rehana smiled.

"It's just in case, Dilly. It's going to be fine. Put it away – DON'T let the girls touch it – OK. Right, let's get a move on," she ordered.

Sensing the danger neither the girls nor the dogs complained. Rehana watched us make our way to the back of the cave where it opened out into a maze of tunnels.

I led the way, carrying Hira, then Elif and Xena with Xabur bringing up the rear.

Years of playing here had taught us all the cliff's nooks and crannies and it was easy for me to thread my way through the maze and onto a secret exit overlooking the hidden pool.

This side of the cliff face was completely obscured from view and allowed me to lead the little procession down to the pool and on to the cave where we were to wait for Rehana's return.

I reckon it took about ten minutes and we waited in silence for another half hour. I used the time to update my diary – desperate to record the reunion with my sisters and how we fled the clutches of the ratmen – one hand resting on the bump of the grenade in my bag – just in case.

32. ... AND FINDING ONE!

Xabur lay at the cave entrance – on guard duty and it was his rising hackles that alerted me that someone was approaching.

Slipping my hand inside my bag, I clasped the grenade, ready for whatever might appear – but it was Rehana – thank God.

"They've set up a road block at the top crossing – from that junction they can see virtually the whole valley," she grimaced.

"But I think I've found a route through," she smiled, before dropping the bombshell. "It's brilliant but we're going to need rope."

In my mind I pictured the large coil of rope and equipment stored in the basement under our house.

"Means going back to the house Reh, it's too risky," I heard the panic rising in my voice.

She nodded – her eyes flashing with determination.

"Yeah you're going to have to help me. It's our only chance."

Sitting in the entrance to the cave, sunlight warming our outstretched legs, Rehana slowly outlined her brilliant, if slightly flawed strategy.

"I've counted eight of them already in the village and we know they've got dogs with them – but," she hesitated before ploughing on, "there's more coming, I've seen them coming across the valley floor from the east – just a few at the moment but there will be more.

"Our only hope is to sneak away without being seen… or smelt."

I knew, from what she'd already
said, that if they held the road junction
and the valley, the only way left was
the river. This lower path that we were
on led straight down to the river and
I guessed why Rehana wanted the rope.

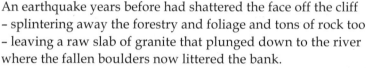

The reason this lower path was
rarely used was that it led nowhere.
An earthquake years before had shattered the face off the cliff
– splintering away the forestry and foliage and tons of rock too
– leaving a raw slab of granite that plunged down to the river
where the fallen boulders now littered the bank.

It was a sheer drop of at least thirty metres.

Rehana explained that with the rope she could lower me over
the drop, then the girls, before climbing down herself. Tracing
the river's edge the strewn boulders would shield us from view.

Following the river could take us across the valley and far
from the village, to reach the path we'd take to the minefield,
then the tunnel, then Turkey.

In my mind I was already there.

It was a brilliant and doable plan – but without a rope it
was hopeless. With little time and no alternatives the decision
was made.

At the prospect of a clear run home with Rehana and my
sisters – I was overjoyed. But as Rehana revealed the next part
of her plan the joy gave way to terror.

"So the girls are safe here – for now," said Rehana, and
looking over at them we realised that Elif was rocking Hira to
sleep on her legs – sitting with her back propped against Xena.

"We'll leave them here with the dogs and you and me will
go back up to the house with this," she grinned, patting her
super-duper rifle.

"I'll set you up with it camouflaged in the branch of the old tree on the corner. From there I can dash to the house and grab the rope. Most of them are looting the market – but if one does stray near or sees me – shoot him. That's an order. Don't hesitate. I'll still have time to make it back and once we drop over the cliff face they'll never catch us. Probably plummet to their deaths with luck."

"Inshallah," I whispered.

"Got it?"

I nodded.

"Good, then let's go," she ordered.

Rehana explained to Elif that we needed to collect some rope for the journey. "You're in charge," commanded Rehana. "Wait here with the dogs. Do not move. We'll be back."

It broke my heart to leave them there – but they were flanked by Xena and Xabur and I was determined to save them, so I went.

Rehana was waiting for me outside at the bottom of the climbing path that twisted back up to the caves above us.

"We'll be quick. We can do this," she urged. "This is our village – our land – it will help us and hinder them. We're warrior women and they're bastards – don't forget that and we'll beat them."

And with that she set off at a run, leaning forward into the climb, her rifle over her shoulder. I struggled to keep up with her.

Determination spurred us on and in no time, panting and doubled over in pain, we stumbled to a halt at the cave entrance. From there it was straight through the caves and up the track to the cliff top.

The tree Rehana had selected was growing out of the cliff face where the ground started to level out.

From the track below it was easy to reach the lower branches and swing high into the canopy – we'd done it often. Two thirds of the way up, branches thicker than my leg reached out towards my house and it was here that Rehana led me.

Unhooking the rifle from her shoulder, Rehana slid it along the branch in front of her before slithering into place behind.

Setting up the tripod and removing the safety catch, Rehana lined up the sights across the open cliff top garden towards our house. She loaded and primed the rifle.

Satisfied she shuffled backwards and nudged me into her now vacant space. Manoeuvring into place behind the gun butt I remembered lying here before, tormenting my brothers or cousins by squirting them with water pistols camouflaged in the branches.

Same difference, I tried to convince myself.

Looking through the sight Rehana had lined up, gave a clear view right across the open ground to the back of the house.

"That's where I'll be exposed. You see anyone other than me – shoot them."

I nodded and she was gone, coiling back down through the branches, slipping to the floor and running swiftly across the open ground.

So far so good. Watching her race to execute her plan I realised it was this that set Rehana apart and made her the legend that she had become.

No sooner had she committed to a plan than it was completed.

She was brilliant – the ratmen wouldn't even know she'd been – and they wouldn't have – if it wasn't for the dogs.

33. DISASTER, DOOM and RATS' BLOOD

I heard them before I saw them. From nowhere a howling nearly startled me out of the tree – they'd clearly picked up Rehana's scent.

A hunting cry. I could hear them but still couldn't see them – they were approaching fast but blocked from my view by the house.

Rehana had already reached the basement as the dogs descended on the house from the orchard side.

They were dancing and howling at the cellar space below the house where Rehana was retrieving the rope.

They couldn't reach her – the trapdoor on the orchard side was shut but their frenzied yowling brought the ratmen to the chase skidding to a halt in their truck and racing up to the house.

I could hear them – doors banging, shouting, dogs barking – where was Rehana? Come on – come on.

Waiting for her to appear. Willing it to work.

I closed my eyes, wishing the rifle were a wand, realising it would take magic to save us now.

Then, emerging from the other trapdoor on the side of the house facing me, Rehana reappeared with rope coiled over her shoulder and hit the ground sprinting.

As the frenzied pack and ratmen were shielded from me by the house, so Rehana was shielded from them and in the confusion I hoped against all hope that the crazed dogs wouldn't pick up the scent of the terrified, fleeing Rehana. But even as the hope flickered alive in my brain, the dogs, who had been beaten to silence by the shouting men, set up another howling chorus and I pictured them straining to the garden.

Sure enough, first one, then two of the monstrous beasts appeared together at the back of the house – eyes on Rehana as she raced for her life across the cliff top.

Loosing the rope from her shoulder as she ran, Rehana flung it over the cliff and I watched it bounce, uncoil and slink to the path below.

Even now, Rehana had found the time to save me and the girls.

Well, I would save her right back. She wouldn't fail. Couldn't fail. But try as I might, levelling the sights on the dogs wasn't possible – the lead dog raced low to the ground like a rocket and was gaining on Rehana who still had only made it halfway across the cliff top.

The look of absolute determination on her face convinced me, against all the odds, that she was going to make it. But even before the dogs had reached her it was over. Screaming round the side of the house raced the ratmen in their truck, screeching to a halt in front of the defiant Rehana.

There were eight of them now – three in the cab and five in the back – the tiniest sob escaped my thoat as Rehana looked directly up at the tree and gave a tiny shake of her head – imperceptible to the ratmen. She was telling me not to shoot.

Imploring me with her eyes to get back to the girls.

Watching the horror unfold beneath me I was frozen with fear. This wasn't part of our plan. What to do? What to do? The question bounced and echoed round my empty head.

I was panicking and wasting time, distracted by what ifs

and why. Why hadn't I run for the rope and left Rehana with the gun – she could have killed them all – for sure. Lining up the sights against the biggest of them I considered taking a shot – but quickly realised that would only make things worse. I didn't have enough time to reload – they would find me and that would be the end of all of us.

Think – think!

Sweat was running down my face, stinging my eyes. Still I did nothing. Still I watched. They were circling Rehana now – like vultures, laughing, taunting her – I couldn't understand what they were saying – Rehana didn't move – just stared ahead into the distance as if she couldn't see them.

That angered the biggest one of them. He was clad, as they all were, in their death-dress. Baggy black trousers, long black tunic, black balaclava. Black, faceless, hollow-eyed crows pecked at Rehana. A swarm of Dementors but together they couldn't pierce Rehana's spirit. She remained undaunted.

Stopping in front of her the bigrat raised his chin and spat in Rehana's face. No reaction. He went to walk past, hesitated and then punched Rehana in the side of the head.

Knees buckling she hit the ground but she didn't complain or cry out. It was as if they couldn't reach her.

The bigrat pulled out his gun. Oh god. He was going to shoot her. What to do? What to do? I couldn't get a clear shot of him…

Two other ratmen dragged her back to her feet by her hair and it was then that one of them recognised her.

"Well well well look who we have here!" marvelled a skinnyrat. "If it ain't the poster girl for the YPJ herself! What a prize."

I could only understand a few of their words – but reaching for his phone I realised, with horror, that Rehana's warrior reputation preceded her.

Brandishing the phone to his friends, proclaiming Rehana's triumphant tally of one hundred slaughtered ratmen, sent them spiralling from anger to frothing with fury.

Screaming and snarling at Rehana I thought they were going to rip her apart on the spot. But the bigrat was clearly in charge and decided to make an example of her and the ratlets squealed with delight.

Chaining the dogs to the truck, the rest of the ratmen produced phones and cameras and chatted excitedly as they wandered towards me and the shade thrown out by the tree, to enjoy the spectacle.

As the bigrat marched Rehana to the centre of the open ground I knew, only too well, what was about to happen. Finally shaking the paralysis of panic I weighed up the situation.

The rest of the ratmen had gathered in a group not far from the lower branches of the tree, stationed between me and Rehana with her executioner.

They were making a show. A show in which Rehana was the star. The bigrat put his hand on Rehana's shoulder, and, his touch triggered a lightning response as she headbutted him, smashing the back of her skull into his face. He screamed in fury as blood spurted from his nose and a trace of satisfaction reached Rehana's lips as she raised her arm in front of her in her trademark victory salute, staring straight at me. She was saying goodbye. Giving me her blessing. Willing to sacrifice herself so I could save the girls.

The blood and fury set the dogs howling again, and as this was being recorded for broadcasting on their sick internet sites, two of the ratmen left the group below the tree and went to quieten the dogs down with a kick and a stick.

It was the first time I had seen the whole pack. They were chained to the back of the truck, which was blocking a clear view. But I got glimpses. I counted four maybe five massive square, black heads, over the back of the truck, ears clipped into sharp points like wolves. Filthy and furious, they snarled and snapped at each other, battered into silence by the ratmen armed with broomsticks. The air was charged with their animal anger. These were undoubtedly the devil dogs I'd heard of.

Take two.

The bigrat jabbed Rehana in the arm with the tip of his dagger and forced her to her knees in front of him, gritting his teeth.

One of the ratlets raced over to stem the blood from his nose – I determined to listen to only one of the thousand screaming voices in my head – Rehana's calm voice. It gave me the sense to form a plan. I could do this.

Staring down the sights of the rifle I saw the look on Rehana's face. Dignified and defiant. Raising the sights upwards I found my target. The swollen face of the bigrat. His nose had stopped bleeding and he was ready to continue his performance.

Yanking Rehana's head back by her hair the bigrat jabbed a

dagger into her throat as he began to spout hatred to the camera.

Rehana winced as the point of the dagger pierced her skin. The red dot of the rifle sight followed my eye as it trailed down

to Rehana's neck and I watched a droplet of blood bubble at the surface and ooze onto the blade.

I was panicking again. FOCUS I screamed to myself and dragged the sight back on target.

I heard the bigrat shout 'Kaffir' ripping the blade away from her throat and gesturing wildly at the avid cameramen grouped below me. The audience bayed and roared their approval – punctuating their screams with cries of "Allahu akbar."

Reaching down with one hand I flipped open the bag on my hip and grasped the grenade.

Placing the ring pull between my teeth I rested the grenade on the branch in front of me. It was time.

Shouldering the rifle butt I squeezed the trigger and watched the little red dot spring to life on the bridge of the bigrat's nose.

Closing one eye and holding my breath I concentrated. The ratmen below me had fallen silent in anticipation of the show.

"Allahu akbar," the bigrat echoed and I realised he was reaching the finale.

Checking the red dot was in position I squeezed the trigger all the way back and fired – nothing.

My heart lurched. A brief second of panic – while the super smart gun checked I was on target – then BOOM! – Even I was shocked as the head of the bigrat exploded off his shoulders.

Without waiting I ripped the pin from the grenade and started counting, one second, lobbing it underarm, clear of the branches, high into the air, two seconds, I watched it spin, flying through the sky then hit the ground and roll to just a metre from the group of rats below me, three seconds, squealing rats, BOOOOOM!

Rat confetti.

34. A GLIMMER OF HOPE

From the corner of my eye I caught Rehana flying towards me drenched in the blood and guts of the bigrat.

Glancing to the truck, I realised the two ratmen on guard-dog duty, terrified by their unseen enemy, had leapt for cover on the floor of the cab. The dogs were creating havoc and for the time being at least, the petrified ratmen were staying put.

The group below the tree had taken the full blast of the grenade.

One had been blown clear and landed ten metres away, nearer the truck. I couldn't tell if he was dead or just dazed. That left four. Three were dead and the one still alive was sitting, screaming at a bloody stump where his leg used to be.

I struggled to take it all in but was snapped back to life by Rehana screaming, "MOVE!" as she raced towards me. Shuffling back off the branch I snatched the rifle and dragged it behind me as I slid down through the tree.

But just as Rehana reached the path the rifle tripod hooked over a branch and stuck fast. Reaching me as I wrestled with it, Rehana tugged me out of the tree by my legs.

"Leave it – let's go," she screamed dragging me in front of her and shoving me on the back into a run.

We made the cave opening in record time, snatching up the rope on the way and automatically sitting to rip off our boots. Keeping them on could drown you when you hit the river as they would fill with water dragging you to the bottom. We could still hear the blood-curdling cries from above, a mixture of pain and fury.

I wasn't sure if the ratmen left alive had even seen which way we'd gone and prayed we'd bought ourselves a little time to escape with the girls.

Looking at Rehana as she wrestled with her boots I realised she was radiant, electrified. She'd resigned herself to death with dignity but was clearly overjoyed to be alive.

"Brilliant plan – just brilliant, Dilly," she said, wreathed in smiles as she started coiling the rope over her arm. "After you," she gestured to the secret water chute. Sitting on the edge, boots on my hands, I swung my legs over the side, grinned at Rehanna and slipped in.

Spinning through the cool dark tunnel, tumbling away from the madness unfolding above me, my brain caught up with itself and eased the terror level coursing through me.

Splashing into the icy water brought me sharply to my senses and, turning on my back, boots clasped to my chest, I kicked out for the bank.

Three seconds later and Rehana plopped into the pool behind me. Hauling ourselves onto the bank a few minutes later, we stood speechless, panting and dripping, before Rehana clapped me on the back and set off for the girls.

Xabur had heard us splashing into the pool, his hackles had warned Elif and there was no sign of the girls when we entered the cave.

But calling to them they appeared from its deep recesses, clearly delighted to see us, wet but in one piece, the river having washed most of the rat gore from Rehana.

Rehana retrieved her rucksack and shouldered it and then grabbed the rope. I picked up Hira and set her on my hip and taking Elif's hand we left the cave and set out for the river.

Xabur led the way and Xena brought up the rear of our little procession as we made our way along the lower track.

It was a wide and open path dropping to the river on one side and banked by the rising cliff face on the other.

Ahead lay a gently sloping bank that wound round the cliff, disappearing down to the drop to the river, which armed with our prized rope, we were planning to descend.

Even if, with the keen senses of that starving pack, the surviving ratmen managed to track us this far – they could never follow us over the edge.

Without a rope of their own they would risk being smashed to pieces, plunging onto the shattered boulders below.

Once we were over the cliff face we had a chance.

We made good progress – running twenty, walking twenty paces so Elif could keep up – Rehana weighed down with all the gear, me carrying a worried, and still silent, Hira.

But we were still quite a way from the finish when we heard them. It was the dogs. And they were gaining on us.

Snatching up Elif, Rehana broke into a run towards the next bend in the track and shelter provided by a fallen boulder.

They were screaming down on us as we raced to the boulder. We had no hope of reaching the drop or the lengthy process of climbing down to the river.

Skidding to a halt behind the boulder I squashed the girls into a crevice and took up a position next to Rehana as she stared over the rock and up the path – waiting for whatever was approaching.

She'd dropped the rope and was rifling through her rucksack, eyes still on the track. She was searching for something. Suddenly I remembered, and snatching her knife out of my bag I thrust it into her hand.

Handing me two more grenades she said, "We haven't got the rifle but if it's just the dogs we stand a chance. Wait 'til they're close, 'til they pass that tree then throw the grenade to land in front of them as they reach that dip." She pointed to the far side of the boulder.

Having witnessed the devastating effects of a grenade blast close up I felt reasonably confident that between us we could tackle the dogs before they got too close.

The prospect of us being ripped apart by those death dogs terrified me and I considered keeping one grenade back for me and the girls – just in case.

Sensing my wobble, Rehana said, "If it's just the dogs they'll come at us in a pack – one grenade will probably do it."

But it wasn't just the dogs.

And they didn't come as a pack.

And for the second time that day I found myself paralysed with fear as our brilliant plan collapsed around us again.

35. ... EXTINGUISHED!

The first dog to round the bend was the fast one – the one that chased Rehana across the cliff top behind my house – and he was still hot on her trail.

He appeared round the bend, racing towards us low to the ground, followed a little way behind by a bigger dog.

Just as they raced into view, a gunshot and a shouted command from somewhere in the trees, brought them both to the floor – where they lay cowering.

Momentarily relieved that they'd stopped, I soon realised that what was coming next was far worse.

The voice clearly belonged to the ratmen who guarded the dogs – they were crashing down the side of the cliff – stumbling through the trees to where the first dogs had guided them and now waited obediently for them, below. There were three of them – each led by a monster dog on a long leash, they plunged and thrashed through the thicket.

Furious and flailing with machetes they hacked a path down

the cliff face. Realising at the same time our plan was hopeless, we snatched up the girls and raced for the drop.

Our only hope left was that their slow climb down the cliff would give us just enough time to get down to the river bank and escape.

It was a long shot.

And as we emerged from the shelter of the boulder we were in plain sight. I don't know what kind of formidable opponent they must have been expecting, one that, with deadly stealth killed their leader and four of their friends.

But I don't think it was the sorry sight of fleeing children and a couple of dogs. Whooping with delight at the sight of their prey they leapt like ninjas from the cliff face and onto the path behind us.

We were trapped. No time to make the climb. Nowhere to go. We turned to face them. Rehana's Raggle-Taggle Army. Walking briskly down the hill towards us – they laughed and whistled and jeered. Holding hands, Elif and Hira stood rooted to the spot next to us. Xabur and Xena slightly in front.

Glancing at Rehana I could see she was calculating. The fall down the cliff side had taken a toll on the ratmen. They sported cuts and bruises and aside from the machetes two of them appeared to have lost or abandoned their weapons en route.

Did she think she could stop the entire pack of dogs and the advancing ratmen with grenades?

Whether she did or not, what she said was, "We're not going down without a fight." The ratmen stopped a short distance from us and marshalled the dogs into a line.

"Run brats, run," they shouted. Run I understood in English – they were excited at the prospect of a manhunt and shook the dogs, baiting and riling them.

We stood fast. Running would only make a better show for

them. They shrugged, disappointed to be denied the thrill of a chase. Then, with one guttural command they set the dogs on us.

Like a tidal wave they surged towards us. A mob of wolves, angry eyes and fangs, screaming down the hill.

Fear had tensed every cell in my body.

This was it – the end and it was all my fault. I couldn't breathe or move – my brain had stalled in fear.

I was watching the approaching pack like it was a television show – but without a remote to turn it off. Seeing them together, there was something familiar. Five of them, the fast one, the three smaller ones, the big one…

Xabur and Xena were ready – slightly ahead of us – the front line – braced for the onslaught. Suddenly, pointing at the descending pack, Elif sobbed, "It's Fluff!"

And sure enough, clearly visible on the collar of the biggest dog as he approached, were threads of familiar red cloth – from the ripped kerchief that Elif had embroidered for him. There was no mistaking it.

These were our puppies – blackened with oil and dirt and crazed with the cruelty they'd suffered since we'd abandoned them.

Sudden horrifying recognition blazed in Xabur at the same time.

And, as Jet closed the gap between us, Xabur sprang forward, landing in his path, throwing his huge head back and howling.

The ratmen laughed at the spectacle. The sport of a struggle to the death amused them and they sat down on the grassy bank to finally enjoy the show we'd denied them earlier.

Any of us the dogs didn't rip to shreds would be shot. As I watched Rehana finger the pin on her grenade behind her back, I knew it was now while the ratmen were distracted by the imminent dog fight and I slid my hand into my bag, reaching for the grenade and smiled down at my sisters.

36. Justice

Turning to Rehana, I nodded.

"Wait for my command," she breathed.

Her voice was drowned out by a deafening howl from Xabur.

Whether it was fear, or love – I don't know. But since that day in the garden Jet had clearly learnt his lesson and I watched as he hit the floor in submission in front of his furious father.

Cowering onto his back and whimpering, Jet offered total subservience to the towering might of Xabur.

For a second I thought Xabur would rip out his throat as he stood snarling over terrified Jet. But certain of his dominance Xabur turned his back on his defeated son and faced the rest of the pack.

With Xena at his side and Jet now on his feet behind them, the three dogs took the chase towards the approaching pack.

Running straight into their midst Xabur braced, raised his huge head and howled his authority again.

The ratmen, unaware of the family reunion being played out in front of them, urged their dogs on.

But the sight of their mighty father and loving mother overwhelmed the dogs, who cried like children and nuzzled Xabur's neck.

It was heart-warming for us to watch. The dogs clamoured for Xabur's attention and forgiveness.

But Xabur had other things on his mind. Lowering his head he fixed the ratmen in his sights.

The look of confusion that spread across their faces in the following seconds, followed by terror, was a real treat for us. Using one of his silent commands, Xabur stilled his joyful pack, and as one they turned to face the bewildered ratmen.

Leaping to their feet the ratmen called to their pack. But it was too late. Allegiances had changed. Love had won the day.

"Run!" I shouted their taunts back at them as Xabur let out a low growl and launched himself at the ratmen.

Horrified and stumbling they set off up the hill but it was pointless. Within seconds Xabur had reached them and as he leapt to rip the throat from the first ratman he brought down, he was overtaken by his loyal pack.

Cheering and clapping with delight we watched the now six-strong pack gaining on the two remaining ratmen as they fled back up the path.

The one with the gun, desperately struggling to unhook it as he ran, tripped and fell, and Jet and Fluff were upon him.

The last was caught by Kiwi, Cherry and Blossom and disappeared in a cloud of fur and fangs that soon blazed red with his blood.

Screams pierced the sky accompanied by the frenzied growling as the pack devoured their prey.

I didn't feel sorry for them. This is what they'd trained the dogs for. It's what they wanted for us. It's what they deserved. We turned the girls away and headed for the drop – the gruesome sound of the ratmen being finished off ringing in our ears. I bet they wish they'd stayed in Britain now.

We walked to the drop in stunned silence. All of us shocked by the savage scenes we'd just witnessed.

Shocked but not sorry. "It's what they deserved," said Elif, echoing my earlier thoughts.

The dogs caught up with us as we were descending the cliff face. Realising our route, Xabur jumped his family further across a ravine then down the cliff face threading through the trees to a low point above the river where they all leapt in.

Our reunion on the riverbank was a happy one. Washed clean by the river they were no longer devil dogs. They were our furry family and they'd saved our lives.

They cried and whined and we hugged and patted them. Delighted to see them safe. Delighted to be alive.

"We'd better get moving," said Rehana. "We need to cross the valley and get back to the tunnel."

"Can't we go home now the dogs have killed all the ratmen?" asked Elif.

"Soon we can," smiled Rehana. "But right now we need to go and find your dad.

"I was with the general yesterday when I got that email with the pictures of your sisters," she told me as we walked on.

"When I showed him and he realised their desperate situation he bribed someone at the Turkish jail to get your dad and brothers' court date moved up. They should be on their way here right now with luck."

We trekked in silence for a while. The sun was still high in the sky but disappearing beyond Lanaco.

The walk was calming. Us and the dogs and the river. You could almost forget we were crossing a war zone.

We made the path that led up to the minefield in good time and the prospect of crossing it for the third time didn't bother me after what we'd been through today.

But as we reached the top of the path the unmistakable sound of trucks forced us to take cover in the undergrowth.

We couldn't see them and hoped they couldn't see us – but the pack of dogs on the path might be a giveaway.

The trucks had stopped not far from us. We could hear doors banging and voices. They could definitely see the pack – would they come closer to investigate? Suddenly Xabur stiffened and pricked his ears towards them.

And then we heard it too, a familiar voice, calling, "Xabur – come boy."

A grin spread amongst us – but it was Hira who spoke first, no longer dumbstruck, "Daddy," she shouted. "My daddy!"

37. THE POMEGRANATE TREE

So here I am – back in the courtyard – in the shade of the pomegranate tree, taking the chance to update my diary.

The courtyard's busy now. Full of my family. My dad and brothers, my sisters and dogs. We're all here – just my mum still missing and hopefully not for much longer.

Looking at my dad, he and the general are studying more of those aerial photographs showing the truck that took her and tracking its path. If anyone can find her, it will be my dad.

The general had collected him and my brothers from the Turkish court this morning and driven them straight to the border.

They were greeted by a waiting YPG patrol when they emerged from the tunnel and armed to the teeth, a convoy of six trucks of

Kurdish fighters set out for Rojava to rescue us.

They had stumbled across us just five minutes into their journey and our reunion couldn't have been any sweeter.

We wept as we embraced. Tears of joy and relief. They looked older but they were alive. All of them. My dad, Nuri, Sela, Azad, Bilal and Baran.

Who was more delighted was hard to tell.

Nuri reached us first, shouting 'Keca Kurda' as he flung one arm round me and the other round the girls. After that he only had eyes for Rehana – and she him – but I didn't mind in the least.

Xabur raced to my dad's side as he scooped all three of us girls into his arms and squeezed us to him.

He sobbed as he held us close and thanked God that we'd been spared. Even Azad wept with joy as he kissed me.

And so it was that we returned in triumph to Lanaco – entering the courtyard, raised aloft on the shoulders of our victorious brothers.

That was a few hours ago. The deafening chants of 'Azadiya Kurdistan' and cries of 'Keca Kurda' for me, Rehana and the girls had faded.

We'd sat, then, in a circle and talked and listened and shared our stories before my dad had been called away by the general to study this new information.

Glancing around the courtyard I took in my family. Hira and Elif playing with Azad and the twins, Seladdin talking and laughing with the YPJ girls Sydrah and Songul and Rehana delightedly showing Nuri the replacement super-duper laser-guided rifle the general had just rewarded her with. The dogs sprawled against the wall next to me, Xabur's head in my lap. I smiled at the murderous beast and used the end of my pencil to pick a lump of goop from the corner of his eye. Rubbing it clean on his fur I resolved not to suck it again.

The general was on the phone and my dad was lost in his own thoughts.

I closed my eyes and replayed the conversation we'd had earlier in my head. "I'm so proud of you, Dilly. You did the right thing. You were so brave, so clever, so Kurdish – my Kurdish girl – you rescued your sisters. Your mum would be proud too," he told me, tears streaming down his face. Before today I'd never seen my dad cry – and now he couldn't stop.

"You symbolise everything we're fighting for – everything we stand for – the right to live freely on our own land in peace.

"You're our future Dilly, you and the girls, your brothers, Rehana," he said, gesturing across the courtyard with one arm pulling me in for a hug with the other.

197

Opening my eyes I stared across at my dad. He was still lost in his own thoughts and having been lost in mine I realised I'd already started sucking the pencil again.

Spitting it out I realised my dad was thinking about my mum and the one missing piece of our family puzzle.

Stuffing the book and pencil back in my bag, I shoved Xabur's nose to the floor and stood up, thinking I'd take my dad a glass of tea, then I thought better of it. Plucking a pomegranate from the tree I decided to give him hope.